SPECIAL MESSAGE TO READERS

THE ULVERSCROFT FOUNDATION
(registered UK charity number 264873)

was established in 1972 to provide funds for research, diagnosis and treatment of eye diseases. Examples of major projects funded by the Ulverscroft Foundation are:-

- The Children's Eye Unit at Moorfields Eye Hospital, London
- The Ulverscroft Children's Eye Unit at Great Ormond Street Hospital for Sick Children
- Funding research into eye diseases and treatment at the Department of Ophthalmology, University of Leicester
- The Ulverscroft Vision Research Group, Institute of Child Health
- Twin operating theatres at the Western Ophthalmic Hospital, London
- The Chair of Ophthalmology at the Royal Australian College of Ophthalmologists

You can help further the work of the Foundation by making a donation or leaving a legacy. Every contribution is gratefully received. If you would like to help support the Foundation or require further information, please contact:

THE ULVERSCROFT FOUNDATION
The Green, Bradgate Road, Anstey
Leicester LE7 7FU, England
Tel: (0116) 236 4325

website: www.foundation.ulverscroft.com

Anne Perry is a *New York Times* bestselling author noted for her memorable characters, historical accuracy and exploration of social and ethical issues. Her two series, one featuring Inspector Thomas Pitt and one featuring Inspector William Monk, have been published in multiple languages. She has also published a successful series based around World War One and the Reavley family. Anne Perry was selected by *The Times* as one of the twentieth century's '100 Masters of Crime'.

You can discover more about the author at www.anneperry.co.uk

A CHRISTMAS RETURN

As the festive season approaches, Charlotte Pitt's grandmamma, Mariah Ellison, is facing Christmas alone. When an unexpected package containing an ominous present is left on Mariah's doorstep, memories are sparked of a Christmas in Haslemere long ago, when her beloved friend Cullen Wesley died and a local villager was brutally murdered. No killer was brought to justice. Now, the unsolved case has resurfaced and Cullen's grandson and sleuth in his own right, Peter, begs for Mariah's help to solve the crime that led to his grandfather's death. Mariah can't resist a friend in need and she returns to Haslemere to investigate the murder and heal old wounds. But evil still lurks in the picturesque village and she'll need all her wits about her to see that justice is done.

ANNE PERRY

A CHRISTMAS RETURN

Complete and Unabridged

CHARNWOOD
Leicester

First published in Great Britain in 2017 by
Headline
London

First Charnwood Edition
published 2019
by arrangement with
Hachette UK
London

A catalogue record for this book is available
from the British Library.

ISBN 978–1–4448–4320–0

Published by
F. A. Thorpe (Publishing)
Anstey, Leicestershire

Set by Words & Graphics Ltd.
Anstey, Leicestershire
Printed and bound in Great Britain by
T. J. International Ltd., Padstow, Cornwall

To all who have the courage
to keep on trying

Christmas was just over a week away. Should Mariah Ellison bother the servants to put up some decorations in her rooms? No one else would see them, unless somebody paid a duty call upon her. Everybody in the family seemed to be away this Christmas, and Mariah was destined to be alone again. She forced from her mind the thought that it might be largely her own fault. She had been, to put it as kindly as possible, a trifle difficult. She had no doubt that, behind her back, it was put in harsher words.

Mariah had left a change of heart rather late. She refused to count years, and had done for some time. In fact, she had stopped rather before eighty. That was more than old enough for any woman. If she had had any sense, she would have stopped at seventy! She knew many women who had. Queen Victoria was in her seventies, but then she could hardly be discreet about that! In fact, being Queen of a quarter of the world gave her very little discretion about anything at all, something for which Mariah did not envy her.

Being no one of any note allowed Mariah all the discretion she would wish for, and more.

She stood up and walked to the outer door of her rooms, and all the way to the front hallway of the main house. It was very grand, very beautiful.

It belonged to her younger granddaughter, Emily, who had married extraordinarily well with her first husband, in fact above herself, in Mariah's opinion. But to be fair, she had made Mariah reasonably welcome, and she lacked for nothing in the way of comfort. Since last Christmas, and her unusual adventure in the Romney Marshes, when she had been obliged to stay with her daughter-in-law, Caroline, and Caroline's new husband, Mariah had appreciated a lot of things more than she had done in the past.

Emily had good taste, and since she had originally married a wealthy man who had died and left her rich, she had the means to exercise it. Mariah had always been satisfactorily cared for, but not on this scale.

The floor was pale marble, but a warm colour, richly veined. The broad staircase swept down from an upper balcony, its wooden banister polished to a sheen, its newel post a work of art. Three blazing chandeliers hung from the high ceiling. The walls were hung with paintings of aristocrats from earlier centuries. In Mariah's opinion it was a good place to put them, far better than in one of the rooms where one spent time, and would be obliged to look at them.

Although the family was away, there was still a good deal of decoration around: holly with bright berries, red and gold ribbons, coloured candles, and in the corner of the hall a beautifully decorated Christmas tree. It was actually very pretty.

There was a quiet cough behind her.

She turned to see the butler standing a few yards away.

'Excuse me, ma'am, but there is rather a large parcel for you. Or rather, medium sized, but extremely heavy. Would you care for me to carry it to your rooms?' he offered.

'Thank you,' she accepted. Usually she carried a stick to assist her in walking. She had done so for years. It was not really necessary, but it was useful at times. It felt like a weapon, more of an attitude than any real service. She was perfectly steady on her feet, but it was good for leaning on now and then, and certainly for poking things, or people. The implication that she needed assistance made Emily's servants more attentive towards her.

'Yes, indeed!' she went on.

The butler picked up the parcel, which seemed to require some effort for him to do so. He carried it carefully across the hall towards the door to Mariah's quarters.

She had hoped there might be a letter for her, or better still, a Christmas card, but her disappointment was almost swallowed up in curiosity as to what this apparently heavy parcel might contain.

She walked behind him out of the hall and along the passage to her own sitting room where he set the parcel down on the table.

'Would you care for me to open it, Mrs Ellison?' he asked. It did look particularly well sealed and was tied with several rounds of string.

'Yes, please.' Her hands were a little arthritic, she would be bound to be far slower than he, and by now she could hardly wait to know what was inside all this paper and string.

The butler produced a small penknife from his pocket, and opened it up to cut through the string, then the paper.

She watched him with fascination. There seemed to be layers and layers of strong, brown paper around whatever it was. But finally the last layer was undone and they both stood staring at a round, dark brown Christmas pudding. It was ordinary, totally traditional, with a flattened leaf of holly on the top. She could smell the richness of it, now that the wrapping was off.

'Very nice, ma'am,' the butler said, looking at the pudding, then up at her. 'I'm just surprised at how heavy it felt. Would you like me to take it to the kitchen, ma'am? You'll be wanting to keep it until the day.'

She frowned. Who on earth would send her a Christmas pudding? There must be a note somewhere. She stepped forward to lift the pudding.

'Good gracious!' she exclaimed. 'It feels like lead. What on earth have they put in it?'

'Indeed it does, ma'am,' he agreed.

Curiosity overwhelmed her. She went to the side-board drawer and took out a knife. She poked the pudding and within an inch or less, met with total resistance.

'May I help, Mrs Ellison?' the butler offered.

She did not need a butler's help to cut a Christmas pudding. She jabbed the knife hard and achieved nothing at all. Whatever was blocking it was absolutely solid.

4

Very gently he took the knife from her and tried his own hand at it. He also got no further than the first inch. He stopped, uncertain what he should do.

Mariah reached out, took the knife from him and determinedly cut a couple of inches away from the original place. She met with the same resistance, and started to knock the pudding off, away from whatever the obstruction was.

The butler stared in amazement as she slowly uncovered a totally spherical ball of lead, about seven or eight inches in diameter.

'What on earth is that?' he asked.

Mariah felt a sudden chill of memory, indistinct, just sadness, and fear. It was absurd.

'It looks like a cannonball,' she said a little tartly. 'Except it is too small to be a real one.' She poked at it again, and then pushed to see if it would roll. It was solid, and too heavy to do more without a considerable effort behind the push.

'Is it one of those ornamental ones?' the servant asked, staring at it, his face creased with puzzlement.

Inside her mind the memory was suddenly complete. That is exactly what it was: an ornamental cannonball, made of lead just as the real ones were. No wonder it was extraordinarily heavy. She stared at it as if mesmerised, while waves of the past engulfed her like a cold sea.

'Are you all right, Mrs Ellison?' he said with concern. 'Would you like to sit down? I'll take this away and fetch you a cup of tea.'

'No!' she said quickly. Then, remembering the

new person she had determined to be, she added, 'Thank you. You might look to see if there is any note with it, even on the outside wrapping. I believe I know where it came from, but I would like to be certain.'

'Yes, of course, ma'am.' Obediently he picked up all the pieces of paper and examined them on both sides, putting them in a neat pile when he had finished. He kept one in his hands.

'Well, don't stand here!' Her voice was tight in her throat. 'What does it say?'

'It's just the postmark of where it's from, ma'am. There's no more.'

She gulped. Her throat was dry. It was twenty years ago now, almost exactly.

'Haslemere?' she asked.

His eyes widened. 'Yes, ma'am, that's exactly what it says.'

'Thank you. You . . . ' She looked at his pale face, so stiff, so earnest. 'Thank you,' she repeated. 'You may take it to the kitchen. Perhaps you would have someone remove the bit of pudding from the outside. If it is edible, you are welcome to it. And have the cannonball put in the garden shed, if you please.'

'Yes, ma'am. Will there be anything more?'

'Yes, if you please, I would like that cup of tea now, and perhaps something with it. Not Christmas cake. It's too early.'

'Yes, ma'am. How about a nice piece of shortbread?'

'That will do very well.' There was no point in asking him not to speak about the cannonball. He could hardly be expected not to mention to the other staff such an extraordinary event, and quite inexplicable to anyone except her. Should she make up something? Better not. One looked ridiculous being caught in a lie, and by a servant! 'Thank you,' she added.

Until the tea tray came from the kitchen she sat in the extremely comfortable armchair in her own room. It was more of a boudoir than a sitting room. She had no need of such formality. But it was all decorated to her own taste, mostly with furniture she had brought with her, old-fashioned, perhaps a little heavy. She clung on to it simply because it was familiar, and because no one else had given it to her. If she were honest, she disliked some of it, and it certainly carried few good memories. But she could not be obliged to Emily for everything! She stared at the window and the pleasant view of the winter trees that lay beyond. Even in the middle of London, there were some startlingly lovely gardens, especially in the spring; this was one of them. Summer was even more beautiful. Roses covered the pergola, now only tangled with bare stems. And there were also peonies, delphiniums, a blaze of colour.

Haslemere. Why on earth had Rowena Wesley sent her a wretched reminder of past tragedy? It could only be Rowena — couldn't it? Cullen was dead. Putting words to it in her mind brought a stab of pain, even after twenty years. Why should she do it? It was totally unlike her. Rowena had been quietly happy, gentle, generous; in other words, the opposite of Mariah.

Tragedy affects people differently. She had no

7

idea what had happened to her old friend in the time between then and now. But if she were happy, she would hardly have sent this absurd and horrible reminder of the past, which in a few days, twenty years ago, had gone from peace, friendship in which the only shadow had been Mariah's private loneliness, and hurled it all into a complete destruction.

Could it be Peter, Rowena's grandson? He had been badly affected by his grandfather's death, following, as it did, so soon after his parents' death in a tragic boating accident. But he had been a child, no more than ten or eleven. She could see his young face in her mind's eye, calm, fair-skinned, steady blue-grey eyes with dark lashes. He would be over thirty now. She remembered his laughter, before it had all happened. The oddest things would amuse him. She had especially liked that, the unexpectedness of it, the new perception of joy in ordinary things.

What sort of a man had he turned into? Could this be his doing? Why would he be in Haslemere anyway? For the anniversary of Cullen's death? Was he there to help Rowena through it?

The tea came and she drank it, and ate the short-bread without even tasting it.

A card came with the last post of the day. There were usually three or four letters, mostly for Emily and her husband, but this close to Christmas there was so much more of it. The footman brought Mariah's to her room.

'Thank you.' She took it with surprise. She always hoped for cards, but at her age, most of her friends were dead. The younger generation did not keep up with their parents' acquaintances. She could not blame them. She had, in the past, found her own family quite sufficient.

She opened the card and read it.

Dear Mrs Ellison,
Please forgive my melodrama, but the situation is very bad. My grandmother is in trouble of a kind you will not need explaining to you. Owen Durward is back in Haslemere, bent on clearing his reputation. We do not need sympathy, however sincere. We need help, from someone who loved my grandfather, and is willing to fight a hard battle, without fear or favour, to save his name now.

You are the only one I know who answers that description.

Prepare for considerable unpleasantness.

But please come,
Sincerely, Peter.

Actually the card was very pleasant, not the usual sentimental seasonal sort of thing, but a classical sketch of a church spire against a darkening sky. It looked both threatening and oddly hopeful: a light against darkness. It was, however, nowhere near as attention-grabbing as the cannonball. To have sent both, he must really want to ensure I go, Mariah thought.

She would go. Of course she would. In her own bleak and hopeless way, she had loved Cullen Wesley.

9

And it was something, at her age, to be needed — not to be taken in as a matter of kindness. An overdose of charity could kill something inside you.

'Thank you.' She looked up at the footman, who was waiting to see if she needed anything further. He was actually a very agreeable young man. His mother should be commended for the way she had brought him up.

'I shall be travelling to Haslemere in the morning,' she told him. 'I would be obliged if you would have Wilkins arrange for me to be taken to the station, and a train ticket acquired for Haslemere. I will not take much luggage, only what I need for a few days.'

'Yes . . . yes, Mrs Ellison. Is everything . . . all right? You look pale . . . ' He blushed, as if he had spoken too personally to her.

'I am perfectly well, thank you. But I have an old friend who is in great need of some assistance, which I may be able to give. Indeed, I thoroughly intend to do all I can.'

'Yes, Mrs Ellison.' He inclined his head, then left the room, taking the tea tray with him.

⋆ ⋆ ⋆

Mariah set out the following morning. The consideration of what to take, how to pack it, indeed how much luggage to travel with altogether, needed a good deal of her attention. It was not until she was sitting in the train that she relaxed. It was a relatively slow one, stopping at several stations, but the faster one required a change, and she did not wish to be carrying her cases or looking for a porter, and hoping that nothing was late. The less trouble the journey was, the better.

She wanted to keep an even temper, not always something she achieved easily or, for that matter, at all. And she needed to give her attention fully to what she planned to do.

She sat in the carriage and stared out of the window at the passing suburbs, with their rows of houses, their dug-over gardens and bare, winter trees. Shortly they were in the countryside, wider-open, softly rolling hills, ploughed earth making the fields look as if they were dark-corded velvet corduroy. Did that mean in French that it was the velvet of the king? Cord-du-roi? An interesting idea.

Really, her imagination was wandering. Memory of all that Haslemere had meant to her was sharp on the edge of her thoughts. She had been in her sixties the last time she had been here. It felt like an age ago. Everything had been so different. Her own son, Edward, had been alive and Mariah had lived mostly with him and his wife, Caroline, and their three daughters. Now the eldest, Sarah, was dead — murdered, no less, something that no one in the family could quite get over — and sometime after that Edward, too, had died.

Did she miss him? In ways, of course. But they were not as close as she would have liked them to be. He reminded her too much of his father. It was not only his height, his voice and appearance, it was his mannerisms as well, and now and then, his attitude.

That was not fair, and she knew it. Edward had never struck her as his father had struck Mariah herself. He had been a good husband to Caroline, even if he had lacked the wit and warmth of her second husband, Joshua, to whom Caroline was now happily married. It was the first time Mariah had admitted that to herself. After all, what was there to approve of in Joshua? He was years younger than Caroline, and an actor, for heaven's sake! Except that he made her laugh . . .

Was all this passing through her mind because she was going back to Haslemere, and having to think of Cullen Wesley again? He had been her own age, his wife, Rowena, was five years younger, and so very comfortably pretty, with her soft face, and gentle manner.

Mariah had never been pretty, even in her youth. She had had what people kindly referred to as *character*. Had they been more honest, they would have said her figure was handsome enough but her face was plain. Youth had lent her a certain bloom, but it was definitely a loan, not a gift. By the time she was thirty she had one strong, healthy son, and a number of miscarriages. She was deeply unhappy. Fear, shame, and a good deal of physical pain had embittered her, and it showed in the lines of her face.

And yet Cullen Wesley had still liked her.

Or had it been pity, because in his way, his sensitivity, he understood something about her?

No! She refused to allow that thought to remain in her mind. Peter Wesley had said his grandmother was in trouble, or was going to be,

12

and Rowena needed Mariah to be there to help her. Softer, more appropriate, more favourite friends would be no use.

Mariah remembered Rowena herself. She had fair hair that curled naturally, and the sort of complexion every woman desired. She even had a dimple when she laughed. In spite of herself, Mariah had liked her.

What would she find this time, when she got to Haslemere? She did not want to think of it, yet it stayed on the edge of her mind for all except brief moments of the journey.

The countryside, which in the summer was so rich and beautiful, now had a wild look. The gold of the harvest fields was reduced to dark stubble, or the land was already ploughed over and sown with winter wheat. The copses of trees that were once in full leaf, billowing green like lost clouds, were now skeletal, black arms stretched upwards towards lowering skies.

There were parts of Mariah's mind that loved the lean beauty of this season. Nothing was really dead, only resting, withdrawn into itself to prepare for spring, and new life again. It did that every year, regardless of the men and women who lived on it, who husbanded it, or not; even of those who defiled it. It had a truth to itself it never lost.

She reached the village station in the early afternoon and for almost an hour was occupied with the business of getting her cases on to the platform and finding a porter to assist her with them, then getting transport the few hundred yards to the largest inn, where she hoped to spend the first night. She must consider what to do. She had already decided that simply to arrive on Rowena's doorstep, with cases, as if she assumed she were welcome to stay, would be both discourteous and embarrassing. She would find her own lodgings and then visit. Even that was not going to be easy. Peter had told her that there was a terrible issue facing them, but it was not his house to invite her into. Quite possibly Rowena knew nothing of Mariah's impending visit.

It was twenty years since it had all happened, when Owen Durward had been accused of the tragic murder of Christina Abbott, but as she walked into the hallway of the inn, still named the Black Bull, as it had been for centuries, it could have been twenty days. The oak panelling was the same, and the beamed ceilings, but small things had changed. The Christmas tree with its ornaments was new. There were new curtains of an unfortunate shade of green. The old ones had been red. Much better.

The host was still Mr Fletcher, noticeably fatter than before. Too much sampling of his own hospitality, no doubt. His hair was receding, and what there was of it was grey, but his face had the same bland satisfaction she recalled from the past.

'Good afternoon, Mr Fletcher,' she said as pleasantly as she could. 'Mrs Mariah Ellison. I have just arrived from London. I hope you can offer me the hospitality of your establishment, for a night or two?'

He took a long, deep breath. Clearly he did

not remember her. But he must have had thousands of guests through this prosperous place since she had last been here. She had no intention of reminding him of her previous stay in the village.

'A single room, Mrs Ellison? Of course.' He smiled. 'You are fortunate. We can offer you one of our best.' He named a considerable price. 'Will that be acceptable, ma'am?'

'Quite,' she said without a flicker. Emily would meet the cost, if that were necessary. Emily had more money than she knew what to do with, and she would approve of this venture. Her only complaint would be that she had not been included in it. But she was away in Paris for Christmas, with her second husband, Jack, a young man Mariah had disapproved of intensely, to begin with. She had thought him a fortune hunter, after the rich widow Emily's money, and far too handsome for his own good, or anyone else's. But she had learned, with patience, that he was actually quite responsible, and as charming to Mariah as he was to anyone else. His patience, actually, not hers, had settled their relationship into an amicable one. But that had all been before she went to Romney Marsh a year ago, and during the course of investigating a woman's murder she had discovered within herself a very different woman from the old Mariah, and one she liked far better.

The room was all that Fletcher had said it would be. It was on the first floor and overlooked the gardens at the back of the building. The windows were mullioned, probably a conceit, but one she quite liked. The little lead strips dividing it into diamonds gave her the feeling of privacy, without losing the light. And at least up here the curtains were still red. The bed was large and comfortable, with plenty of covers.

She was glad to unpack the few belongings she had brought. She certainly did not need a maid for so little, and more importantly, she had no wish to bring a maid with her on what was an acutely personal visit, digging up a past that might prove painful and possibly embarrassing. Now that she was here, she was full of misgiving. If Rowena were in trouble, what on earth use would Mariah be? She had accomplished nothing before! Cullen was still dead. Christina Abbott was still dead, poor child. Presumably her death was also still unsolved.

After she had washed her face, tidied her hair and composed herself, it was nearly four o'clock. She would go downstairs and have afternoon tea. If spoken to properly, there were always servants who would inform one of the local news and events — gossip, if one cared to use the term. She must learn all she could before calling upon Rowena, and presumably Peter.

She went downstairs to the withdrawing room. It was very cosy, even at this time of year. There were Christmas decorations of red candles, garlands of leaves with ribbons wound through them, and pine cones with holly and a dusting of tinsel and silver powder of some sort. It was cheerful, and not too exuberant.

She seated herself at one of the small tables and ordered a pot of tea and a plate of toasted crumpets with butter and honey. All very delicious. It would fortify her for the decisions she must make.

While she was waiting for the maid to return with her tray, she looked around the room. There were several other ladies present. Two sat together and talked quietly. One sat alone, reading a newspaper. Perhaps it was the court news, or fashion she was looking at. One would hope it was not some of the unsavoury tittle-tattle that the less reputable papers held — so she was told.

A young man came in. He glanced around, and then chose a seat facing the door. Possibly he was waiting for someone.

Mariah received her tea and crumpets and for several minutes lost herself in complete enjoy-ment of the crisp delicacies, soaked in butter and honey, and the hot, fragrant tea. It was quite deliberate. She would have to face the truth soon, but a few more moments of indulgence would strengthen her for it.

Another young man, thinner and darker than the first, came in and sat down, also alone. He glanced at the man who had come in before him, nodded a little curtly, and began to write something with a pencil in a small notebook. A few moments later he was joined by a third young man.

The maid came back in. 'Is your tea all right, ma'am?' she asked politely.

'Excellent,' Mariah said graciously. 'It looks as if you have more customers. There seem to be several young men here, alone . . . ' It was not quite a question, but she hoped it would elicit an enlightening comment.

'Yes, ma'am,' the maid nodded. 'I think they're all from newspapers and the like. Never know whether they're friends or rivals to each other. One minute they're speaking, the next they're not.'

'Good gracious. Is there so much to write about in Haslemere?' Mariah feigned incredulity but she also felt rather fearful.

'Oh, yes, ma'am.' The maid bit her lip. 'I'm afraid you've come at a . . . a funny time.'

'You will have to tell me.' Mariah blinked. 'I'm afraid I am not from here, and I didn't know that . . . '

'It happened a long time ago, ma'am.' The maid nodded again, smiling. 'I was a babe in arms, but my ma told me about it.'

Mariah drew in her breath. This was the very subject she needed to learn about but she knew she must be very careful. 'Indeed? Then what can these young men want now?'

'It was terrible, ma'am. No one's really forgotten it. A young girl, just fourteen years old, she was. Christina was her name. She was taken . . . '

'You mean she was . . . ill?' Mariah pretended ignorance.

'No, ma'am. Taken away, kidnapped. It was terrible.' The maid lowered her voice. 'They found her body. It was unspeakable what they done to her. A man were arrested, but when 'e went to trial, they found 'e wasn't guilty. They never got who really done it.'

'Do they have him now, then?' Mariah said innocently, but there was a chill inside her, a sense of foreboding that almost choked her voice. The girl must have heard it in her.

'No, ma'am. I didn't mean to upset you. I'm terribly sorry. I shouldn't be upsetting guests. Mr Fletcher'll have my job . . . '

'No he won't!' Mariah said sharply. 'I asked you a question and you very civilly answered me. I would be less than human if I did not think the matter very tragic indeed. But why does it arise just now, so many years later?'

''Cos 'e's come back, ma'am.'

'He? Who has come back?'

'Dr Durward, ma'am. Him as was accused wrong. 'E wants to prove as 'e didn't do it, even though 'e was found not guilty. Least that's what everyone is saying. It's raking up all sorts o' memories, an' upsetting folk just before Christmas, an' all.'

'Indeed.' Mariah kept her voice as level as she could. So Owen Durward was going to rake it all up again. He had been tried and found not guilty. That meant he could never be tried for that hideous crime again, no matter what was turned up now. But why? In heaven's name, what good would it do him, or anyone else, to raise such terrible ghosts?

More memories came back to her, ones she had tried to force into oblivion. There had been all kinds of accusations, some against Rowena, not of course that she had had anything to do with Christina's death. Cullen had been the best lawyer in the area of several towns and villages.

He had been retained to defend Durward, and had worked hard on the case.

Then quite out of the blue, he had told Durward that he was unable to continue. Durward had been furious. He had claimed that Cullen's behaviour was appalling. To refuse to continue at this late stage, just before the trial was due to begin, was an unforgivable prejudice against him.

That evening Cullen Wesley had had a fatal accident in his study at his house. A bookcase had toppled over, knocking him to the ground. An ornamental cannonball, extremely heavy, had struck his head. He had never regained consciousness.

Another lawyer had been found for Durward, and three weeks later he had been acquitted of all charges.

Then the gossip about Rowena had begun. Durward was a good-looking man, after a fashion, and more than one village woman had set her cap at him — to no avail. Rowena had had friends, but she had had enemies as well. Gossip was unkind. Mariah was still stunned, and ashamed at her own misjudgement of it.

Rowena's son had died some time before all this. Her grandson, Peter, had been a child. And Cullen Wesley was dead. Quiet, generous, witty Cullen was gone, all except for memories of him so sharp they hurt, so full of loneliness that even now Mariah felt the tears well up in her eyes.

What on earth must Rowena have felt? And still feel all over again now!

This must be why Peter had sent for Mariah.

Why Mariah? Because even though he had been only ten years old at the time, in his own way he'd known that Mariah cared. Please heaven, he did not know how much, or in what manner!

He did not need reason. The trial was over. Durward was pronounced *not guilty*, and Cullen was buried in the local churchyard. Only Rowena was left to be hounded by newspaper reporters, and nosy, cruel people who stilled their own dreams of loneliness or failure by waking old stories to haunt other people.

Mariah Ellison had had her own taste of rage, humiliation and pain too fierce to bear, too strong and too close to escape, except by the mercy of death.

But that was an old story, the humiliation had been at the hands of her husband, not the community, and although it lent Mariah sympathy to Rowena's plight, it had nothing to do with this.

'Thank you,' she said to the maid.

'You all right, ma'am?' the girl asked again. She must have seen the tears on Mariah's cheeks. 'Can I get you another cup o' tea? Fresh, like?'

She did not really want any more tea, but none of this was the girl's fault. She would feel better if she could do something.

'Thank you. That would be most kind.'

Having more tea was not only calming, it gave her a good reason to remain in the room and very quietly, very discreetly, listen to some of the

21

conversation around her as another couple of ladies came in and were obliged to find a table closer to Mariah's, and therefore offering her an opportunity to overhear their exchanges in some detail.

Perhaps it was necessary, but it was a mixed blessing. Gossip was at least entertaining, but only if it did not involve oneself, or the people one cared about. Then it was painful. Mariah had been indulged in her displays of temper, ever since her husband had died. She had never dared argue with him, even less offer any criticism. She had lied for so long about the nature of her marriage, even to herself, that it had come as something of a relief, this last year, to be able to acknowledge it. But that was very far indeed from speaking of it to others. There lies must be upheld, always! For others to know would be unbearable.

But the knowledge within herself had made her see a different side to many arguments, a softer and far more complicated one. It also made her see the poison of gossip.

Now she heard it from the table next to her.

'Of course, you never can tell,' the fairer haired of the two women said, shaking her head. 'One would have thought, to look at her, that she was one of the most respectable of women.'

'And happy,' her darker companion added sagely. 'It's always easier to be good when you're happy.' She nodded, agreeing with herself.

'A good man, Cullen Wesley,' the fair woman pursed her lips. 'Just goes to show!'

'Show what?'

'Why, that appearances can be deceiving! Perhaps he wasn't as interesting as one would assume?'

'Or he had a wandering eye himself?' The fair woman leaned forward a little to confide. 'There was another woman staying with them, you know? Perhaps there was more to that than met the eye also?'

'Rubbish! She was as plain as a cabbage, and with a temperament like vinegar.' The second woman's brief gesture of the hand dismissed the very idea.

Mariah froze. Was that really how people saw her? A cabbage? A boiled vegetable with vinegar? The pain of the idea was almost numbing. She refused to think that Cullen had seen her like that. It was unbearable.

'I thought she was quite clever,' the fair woman resumed. 'Pretty can become tedious after a while. Like blancmange. Nothing really to it. Every mouthful is the same.'

'Saves you having to think,' her friend pointed out its virtue.

Mariah ached to join the conversation, with a remark about vinegar perhaps, or stale food that has been left too long in the larder and has turned sour.

They would be affronted, and demand to know who on earth she was.

'The cabbage,' would be the reply.

But she was not here to pick quarrels, only to help Rowena. Clearly it was going to be very difficult. There were people whose tongues could lacerate, and neither truth nor mercy would still them. It had little to do with fact, and everything to do with their own incompleteness that drew them to such opinions.

She rose to her feet, leaving aside the last crumpet, and walked out of the withdrawing room and up to her bedroom. She did not even glare at the women as she passed them. She must wipe from her mind their very existence. What she had heard was nothing more than a means to impel her forward. This evening she would plan. Tomorrow she would visit Rowena. If it was not raining, the house was within the distance she could walk. Actually, in the last year, since visiting Romney Marsh, she had felt stronger and fitter. Her cane was a weapon, not an assistance to weariness or uncertain balance. She had no need of it. But now she was going to battle with her wits, not any physical accoutrements. Her tongue had always been her sharpest and most agile weapon. She wished now that she had had the courage to use it to defend herself against her husband's abuse. Cowards don't like to be faced down!

He had beaten her but in her fear and humiliation, she had not fought back. It was her self-disgust at being unable to do so that had imprisoned her all these years.

Well, she was free now! And she would fight against Durward, and anyone else who chose to get in her way. All the misery of past battles lost could be assuaged if she won this time. But she must be more than angry, more even than brave: she must be clever. First thing in the morning, after breakfast, she would go to see Rowena.

Never mind old memories and any sense of embarrassment.

⋆ ⋆ ⋆

The morning was bitterly cold. It was dry, thank goodness, but the wind had an edge like a freshly whetted knife and Mariah decided it would be unwise to walk. Finding transport was not difficult. The innkeeper knew all the local tradesmen and providers of a dozen different services.

The carriage, when it arrived, exactly on time, was little more than a gig, but it was quite sufficient. The driver assisted her up and spread a blanket over her lap.

It was a short journey, not more than a mile at most, but very pleasant. The village had barely changed since she was last here, perhaps only a new shop or two on the High Street. There were garlands on some of the doors, brightly painted notices wishing people a happy Christmas.

Of course all the front gardens of the houses were almost bare, but laurel bushes and holly were in full leaf, and here and there other evergreens. It all looked so comfortable, and ordinary, it was as if nothing violent had ever happened, no hatred, certainly no murder.

The obliging coachman set her down just outside the Wesley house. It was named Seven Elms, although to her knowledge there had only ever been five, and one of those was now gone.

She thanked him and paid him generously. She might want him in the future, if this

continued. And since enjoying Emily's hospitality, she had become much less careful in her use
of money. She spared a moment to thank Emily,
in her mind, and to stare at the handsome front
of the house. Twenty years had not changed it.
The window frames had been repainted, but in
the same clean white. The vines around the
dining-room window were taller but, bare of leaf
for the winter, they looked much the same. The
roofs were all the same immaculate slate, and
the fine weathercock was still very slightly
askew.

She forced the memories away, deep into her
mind, both the laughter and the pain. She
opened the gate and went up the paved path,
knowing in advance where the unevennesses
were, as if she had walked it only days ago. At the
front door she climbed to the porch and pulled
the bell rope, then stepped back, as was only
good manners.

The wind whined in the bare branches of the
trees and rattled a loose twig against the side of
the drain-pipe.

The door opened and an elderly manservant
stood on the polished floor inside.

'Yes, ma'am?' he said without any recognition
at all. His face was round and scrubbed-looking,
and there was a tiny cut on his chin, as if he had
been careless or too hasty when shaving.

Mariah swallowed. 'Good morning.' She did
not know his name. If he had been here twenty
years ago, she did not remember him. 'I am an
old friend of Mrs Wesley's and I have come some
distance to visit her,' she said. 'Would you be

kind enough to tell her that Mariah Ellison has called?'

'Yes, ma'am, but I doubt she will . . . be well enough to see you.' His face was almost expressionless. Just in case Mariah was telling the truth, he kept a degree of civility, but it was clear he doubted her. 'If you would be kind enough to wait, ma'am, I shall enquire.'

'I am not waiting on the step in the cold, Jenkins!' she said tartly. They had had a footman called Jenkins, though whether it was this particular one or not she didn't know. His hair was thinning. He might have looked different twenty years ago. And better!

'Mr Jenkins left, ma'am,' he said bleakly. 'But I suppose you had better come inside. It is a most inclement day.' He stepped back and allowed her to enter the foyer and then the hallway. There was a very pleasant settle, a hard, carved wooden bench, rather like a church pew, near the stairs. She walked over to it and sat down.

The man closed the front door, bowed to her very slightly, then went upstairs to see if Rowena would receive her.

This could be awkward.

The room was familiar in all its details. Nothing she noticed seemed to have changed since she had left in such unhappiness twenty years ago. The pictures on the walls were all sea and cloud scenes in the hallway, and, she remembered, all gentle slopes of hillside, trees and wildflowers in the sitting room. These were Rowena's taste, the comforts of long-established land. The wilder ones elsewhere, eyes travelling

27

to the horizon, were Cullen's. From what Mariah could see, Rowena had not moved any of them.

Was that comforting? Or disturbing? Mariah thought the latter. But then she had not wanted to remember anything of her own marriage. She had created a fiction around it, like the protective scars around a wound. Except that they were supposed to fall away of their own accord, once the wound was healed and the new skin grown over it.

Would that ever happen? One day . . .

The wind rattled bare shrubbery branches against the glass. It was the only sound.

Then the footman returned.

'I'm sorry, Mrs Ellison, but Mrs Wesley is not feeling well, and is unable to receive callers today,' he said quietly. He looked very faintly flushed, as if the remarks were not his own.

Mariah knew it was a refusal, not a reason. Rowena was either recalling their less happy associations, the occasional disagreements, or else she was simply too frightened to order her thoughts at all. Neither was an acceptable excuse.

'I am most sorry to hear that.' Mariah measured her words with care. She tried to take the irritation out of her voice, even out of her eyes. He must not sense that she was perfectly aware of the lie. 'It is particularly sad to be ill at Christmas. I think perhaps you are new here? I spent many happy times visiting Mrs Wesley in the past. I had cause to think of her particularly this year. I live in London, you know?' she went on quickly. It was a rhetorical question, not wishing an answer. 'I came on the train to visit Mrs Wesley. It is a time of the year of which we have many memories together.'

The footman struggled for something fitting to say, and failed to find it.

'I am staying at the local inn,' she continued. 'And will do so, in the hope that some time very soon Mrs Wesley is well enough to receive a visit, even if it is a brief one. Please be kind enough to tell her that I am very loath indeed to come this way and not at least have a few minutes with her.'

'Yes, ma'am. I will give her your message.'

Mariah glanced at the window, and the leaves bumping the glass in the rising wind. 'Can you tell me if it is raining?' she asked. 'I would appreciate your hospitality if it is. I prefer not to walk back and get soaked.' She hoped that he understood that she intended to remain.

'Yes, ma'am.' He hesitated. 'Perhaps you would care for a pot of tea, before you return?'

Mariah smiled. 'How thoughtful of you. Indeed, I would be most grateful.' She sat down again before he could change his mind.

The tea was brought and she was shown into the familiar sitting room, with all the pictures she remembered, the bookcases with Cullen's books. There were new curtains, flowered ones. She preferred the old, warm brown velvet.

She was halfway through the tea and light biscuits she had been brought, and wondering how to continue her stay and persuade Rowena to see her, when there was a considerable activity

29

at the front door. She heard it open and close, the sound of footsteps, voices, more footsteps moving rapidly, and then silence. No one came into the sitting room.

Was Rowena really ill, and they had sent for the doctor? How unfair that Mariah had assumed that she was hiding. She could not even apologise without admitting she had thought it a lie.

Then the door opened and a young man came in. He was tall with thick fair hair and an easy smile. He looked perhaps thirty.

He did not seem in the least surprised to see her there, and walked straight over towards her without excuse for intruding. He held out his hand.

'Mrs Ellison?' It was more an affirmation than a question. She did not know him. The footman must have told him her name.

He smiled very briefly, and there was something vaguely familiar about it, a tug at the memory.

'Peter Wesley,' he said briefly. 'I was only ten when we last met. I have probably changed rather more than you have. I'm so glad you came. May I join you?' He sat down opposite her without waiting for her reply. 'They're bringing some tea, and I hope something a little more robust than those biscuits.' All the time he was speaking his eyes were searching her face.

'I have grown older, too,' she said rather more waspishly than she had intended. 'But I am still perfectly well and able to put up a fight.'

His face lit with a wide smile of relief. 'There

isn't really anyone else I can rely on,' he admitted. 'I'm afraid it's going to be rather nasty. You see, this is the twentieth anniversary of Grandfather's death, and damned Durward has decided to come back to the village and clear his name. He can only do that by raking the whole tragedy up again, and condemning Grandmother at the same time. They can't both be telling the truth . . . '

She glared at him. 'Are you suggesting there is some doubt about who is lying?' she demanded.

He smiled again. It was so charming and sudden it was as if he were defending himself against her. Perhaps he was. He had been a child when they had last met, and a child suddenly bereaved, at that.

'I'm sorry.' She surpassed herself by saying it aloud. 'Of course you don't believe Durward. And I am of no use to you if I don't face the facts that we have no proof yet, or you would not have requested I come — especially not in such a . . . melodramatic manner.'

He coloured faintly, but it showed on his fair skin. 'I wanted to be certain of gaining your attention . . . '

'You succeeded.'

'Thank you.'

Before he could say anything further, the footman returned with fresh tea and a large plate of toasted crumpets. Peter thanked him profusely and began to eat even before Mariah poured the tea for him.

'You haven't spoken to Grandmother yet, have you?' He asked it as a question, but it was really

31

a statement of fact.

She realised that the first sound of the door had been his arrival, then the space in time between that and his coming into the sitting room had been his going upstairs and speaking with Rowena. He must know already that she had refused to see Mariah.

'What did she say?' she asked, stepping around the explanation between this and his previous comment.

He looked down, then up at her with apology in his face. 'She doesn't want to see you. She knows you will fight . . . unless you have changed entirely, which I am trusting you haven't?'

'I haven't.' She did not elaborate. Of course she had! She was twenty years older, stiffer and more easily tired. But there were other ways in which she had changed also, over things that had hurt deeply, but had also healed. Circumstances totally outside her control, other people's tragedies, had forced her to acknowledge that her husband had abused her in ways that even now she found too painful to put into words. But finally she had realised that her humiliation at his hands was his sin, not hers. Nor was she alone in such an experience. She could not speak of it to anyone else, but the simple knowledge that she was not unique allowed her to thaw the iron-hard ice inside herself.

And last year, by herself, she had solved the mystery of someone's death. She had found justice for a woman she had begun by loathing, and ended by admiring more than anyone else she had known, a woman whose passion for life had warmed her ever since. Even though the woman was dead, the light of her living had not faded.

The changes in Mariah need not alter anything in what Peter Wesley wished of her.

'So this wretched man has returned to Haslemere?' she said.

'Yes. I don't think any of us foresaw that happening. And, of course, the place is hopping with newspaper reporters like an old dog with fleas!'

'A delightful analogy,' she commented drily.

'I'm so glad you've come!' He said it with warmth, as if he really meant it, and his smile went all the way to his eyes.

Mariah was annoyed with herself for responding to it, but she felt the irritation easing out of her in the same sort of way one smiles automatically in the sun. 'Well, we'd best be thinking clearly,' she said. 'The only way we can mend the situation now is to find the truth, and prove it.'

They sat in silence for several moments, and then an awful fear came into her mind. The silence grew longer. There was no point in running away from it. She took a deep breath. 'Peter, are you afraid that the truth is worse than this suspicion, and that your grandfather refused to defend Durward out of spite, because of some affair with your grandmother? Because that is what the worst gossips are saying. And it is what they will all believe, if we don't prove them wrong.'

'I don't believe it,' he answered quietly. 'But I

have no idea how to prove anything different.'

Her mind raced. She thought of all the conversations she had ever overheard from her other granddaughter, not Emily, but her sister Charlotte, who had married a policeman, one who solved murders. Her mother had encouraged her to marry such a man, possibly because she had refused to marry anyone else. Her father, Edward, Mariah's only son, had been appalled, but had given in.

Actually, the marriage had turned out extraordinarily well. It was one of a few matters in which Mariah had been delighted to be proved wrong. It was unusual only in that she had admitted it.

So what would a policeman do now?

She sniffed. It was a most unladylike gesture, but she was unaware of it.

'Can you think of a more practical alternative?' she asked Peter.

Peter remained silent for some time. 'No,' he said at last. 'I believe the truth is that Durward kidnapped Christina Abbott and then killed her, just as he was charged. I believe Grandfather somehow knew that, and because he did, he couldn't lie to the court, nor could he tell them. That was why he wouldn't continue with the case. Durward was entitled to a lawyer who could at least tell himself he believed Durward's denial. But then that's what I want to believe. I know enough of the law, Mrs Ellison, to be aware that, guilty or innocent, everyone has the right to be tried in court, and have a lawyer defend them. Sometimes the police are wrong.

34

Quite often they have some of the truth, but not all of it.'

'Indeed,' she nodded. 'And they are no longer investigating the case of Christina's death. In fact, since Durward was tried and found not guilty, he cannot be charged again.'

'Then what can we do?'

'Being charged is not all that matters.' She was thinking as she spoke. 'What are we most concerned about?' She answered her own question immediately. 'That poor Rowena will be tried by public opinion, and on a bit of evidence she will be found guilty, with no trial and no one to defend her.'

Peter winced, and his face clearly reflected his pain.

'So we will attack Durward the same way!' Mariah said rashly, hearing her own voice filled with conviction, and wondering if she had lost her wits. Peter looked so like Cullen at that age, or a little older. That was when Rowena had married him and Mariah had married her own husband. Within weeks, Mariah had known it was the mistake of her life. Perhaps it had always been Cullen she loved . . .

Now she was an old woman, and he was long dead. But maybe she could still save his name, his memory, and save his widow and his grandson from grief. They should remember him as they believed he had been, and as she had never doubted he had.

'We must think!' she said fiercely, before Peter could argue. 'It is a perfectly justifiable cause. If Owen Durward has come back to Haslemere to prove his innocence, then the only way he can do that is to prove someone else guilty!'

'Yes,' he agreed. 'But guilty of slander, not of killing Christina.'

'Someone killed the poor child! If it was not him, then who?'

Peter said nothing.

'It was Durward,' she insisted. 'He can't have come back to prove his innocence, because the court already cleared him, the more fool they.'

'Then why is he here?' Peter asked.

She took a deep breath and tried to keep her voice level. 'He is trying to show that Cullen should have defended him. It was his pulling out at the last moment, after accepting to do it, that cast the shadow on Durward. He won't want that case opened again. He will want to blame your grandmother for Cullen's withdrawal from the case. If she were at fault, then Cullen's withdrawal had nothing to do with Durward's guilt. That is all he needs to prove: that he was the victim of a weak man's need to defend his wife's foolishness.'

Peter bit his lip, frowning a little. 'You make it sound simple, but it isn't. Most of the people who'll think about it, write about it now, never knew him. They don't know how far that was from what he was really like.' He looked crushed, as if he could see the embarrassment, the humiliation already.

'I know,' Mariah agreed quietly. 'I don't think it will be easy, but if we don't find the truth, this will never be finished. Your grandmother will never be able to go down the street with her head high, knowing she wasn't wrong, and Cullen wasn't either.' Then the anger boiled up inside her again at the thought of Cullen being slandered like that. 'There's no one who can or will fight for them except us!' She stared straight at Peter, meeting his eyes.

He did not look away. 'Have you any idea where we can start?' he asked.

Her mind raced. She had police in her family. She had at first dismissed her granddaughter's husband as some kind of servant, a person who should go round to the back door, the tradesman's entrance. She would be ashamed of that thought now, if she had the time. He was actually quite clever — no, very clever. What would he do?

Peter was staring at her, the hope still in his eyes. Why on earth had he thought Mariah was the one who had either the courage or the intelligence to solve this? She was not going to be able to live up to anything that he believed of her.

He hadn't! He had just thought she was the one who loved them enough to try, and the fierceness of temperament not to give up. He probably thought she wasn't afraid of anyone. A ten-year-old boy! How could he ever imagine the terror she had lived in all her married life?

She forced it to the back of her mind. No one else must ever know — not ever! Especially not Peter.

'The police must have investigated the kidnap, and then the murder,' she said levelly, as if she really knew what she was talking about. 'If they had not had some sort of evidence against Durward, they would not have charged him, and there would never have been a trial. Someone has to know all about it.'

Peter bit his lip. 'I doubt that the constable will be able to tell us anything. He's relatively new here. Only ten or eleven years.'

'I wasn't thinking of police,' she answered. 'We need someone who doesn't have a vested interest in justifying what happened, or failed to happen.'

'Everyone who was here then had some part in it,' he pointed out. 'They all remember it as they want it to have been. I don't wish to sound sceptical, but it's natural to want to have done the right thing, and to rewrite it all a little bit in your mind.'

'Then I think we have to — ' She hesitated, trying to find the right word; she must get Rowena to face forward and pull herself together! But that was probably not a sentiment Peter would agree with.

He smiled with a dry, twisted humour. 'Get Grandmother to fight beside us?' he suggested.

Mariah let out her breath slowly. 'You have put it rather well.'

He finished the last piece of crumpet. 'I'll go and tell her.' He stood up and walked over to the door, then stopped, turning back to look at her. 'By the way, would you like to stay here, or do you prefer it at the inn? You might remember something useful there, in peace. On the other hand, you could help Grandmother stay resolved if you were here. She can prevail over me, if she tries hard enough. Nobody ever prevails over you, if you've got your mind set.'

'Humph! Do they really prevail over you?' She looked at him with a hint of disapproval.

'Perhaps I should put it differently. She will try with me. She wouldn't dare to with you.' Then he gave a sudden, charming smile and opened the door. 'I shall tell her you are staying. You have come to stand beside her, for old times' sake. Loyalty in times of trouble, and all that. She's enormously grateful, Mrs Ellison. I think it's going to be a very great deal of trouble.' His smile vanished completely and he went out and closed the door quietly.

Mariah sat alone for some time. The footman came in and added a few more coals to the fire, and a log of apple wood from the pile at the side of the hearth. She thanked him. She knew that she must wait until Peter had persuaded Rowena to participate in the battle. Mariah could not help. She would be too blunt, and maybe make Rowena withdraw altogether. Then it might take days, even weeks to change her mind. That would be too late. Durward would have made his case — and won.

She hated that man with a fierceness that drowned her. He had not only killed Cullen, he was determined now also to ruin all that was left of him, his family and his reputation. Why? For his own survival? And perhaps the need to destroy a man so much better than he was himself?

She understood hate, and anger you could not control. She did not want to bring back those days to her mind, for any reason. The scars on her body faded with every passing year. Old shame did not heal so easily. But the scars to her mind were only memory. Were there scars on her soul? That lay within her own control, at least at some point. Wasn't that what Christmas was supposed to be about, really? Trees, cards, ornaments, pictures, even gifts, were all trivialities added on top, sometimes so much that the real gift was lost. It was about healing, forgiveness.

She remembered some curate giving a sermon, a long-necked young man with a ridiculous name, like 'Chicken' or something of the sort. She had been young herself then. He had reminded his listeners, passionately, that forgiveness meant having all past wrongs lifted from you, all debt, all stain, all guilt. It also meant forgiving those who had offended you, or perhaps more difficult, offended those you loved. And it did not depend in the slightest upon whether you believed they were sorry or not.

She had wanted to argue with him. Now in her old age, she understood.

The demand for justice was the same. Then think, can you afford it for yourself, or is it really mercy that you need?

Usually sermons were boring, something to be endured with as much grace as possible. But there were a few, a very few, that remained in the mind all life long.

She must defend Rowena, and to a degree Peter, but not out of hatred for that miserable wretch Durward.

Of course, if it turned out Durward was guilty,

that was another matter!

The footman came and removed the dishes.

'I would suggest a walk, ma'am,' he remarked conversationally. 'But the wind is bitter.'

'Thank you,' she said absently. 'I am awaiting Mr Peter's news of how Mrs Wesley is.'

'Yes, Mrs Ellison. He informed me so. He asked me to have the spare room made up for you. Shall I send the gig to fetch your baggage from the inn?'

She had packed her belongings in hope, then felt she was tempting fate, but she had left them as they were, neatly, with cases closed, because she was impatient to be on her way, and she must not keep the carriage waiting.

'Thank you,' she accepted. 'That would be most agreeable.'

Peter eventually returned looking weary, but pleased with himself.

'She is up and ready to receive you,' he told her. 'If you don't mind my saying so, I think you should avail yourself of the opportunity, just in case she changes her mind. She's very . . . hurt by all of this.' His face tightened, as if he could feel the pain himself, and perhaps he had done. 'Many people who used to be friends have turned against her. She's terribly isolated here. I come when I can, but it isn't so often. She won't leave, because Cullen is buried in the village graveyard. And this was his house, and where they were so happy. She doesn't have the strength to start again, somewhere new where she knows nobody.' He shrugged. 'Sometimes village gossip stays in its own place, but it only

41

needs one person to travel, stay with a friend or a relative, and the whole thing spreads and starts over.' He gave a very slight smile. 'And she wants to run away sometimes, but it passes. Why should she? This is her house, her garden that she's loved and tended for fifty years. Most of it is actually her creation.'

Mariah stood up, waving away his hand offered to help her. 'And why on earth should she let those beasts drive her out of her home?' she challenged. 'It only looks easier to run away sometimes. It isn't really. And anyway, after the filthy newspapers have raked up the whole thing again, where would she go? Ireland? America?' She did not bother to wait for an answer. It was not really a question.

He reached the door before her, in time to open it, then followed her along the hall and up the wide, shallow stairs without speaking again.

Rowena's bedroom was where it had always been, at the back of the house overlooking the garden, which had grown up and matured in the last twenty years, and was even more beautiful. The elm trees now shaded the lawn, or would do, when they had leaves again.

Rowena herself was sitting on the large bed, wearing a house gown of gentle colours, like a pile of fallen petals. She had always been a pretty woman. Her hair was still thick and waving softly, but the colour had faded out of it, as it had from her face. Even though she had no more lines or wrinkles, she looked older than Mariah. The tiredness and the fear were deep inside her, and too real to hide.

It was not the time to pay silly compliments, and not something Mariah had ever done, even when the time would have been perfect.

'Good morning, Rowena,' Mariah said, and sat down on the chair by the side of the bed, very possibly where Peter had sat when he persuaded her to face the battle. 'I am sorry it has taken me this long to visit you.' She had decided to get the apology over immediately. There was no purpose in mentioning that Rowena had not visited her either. It was all beside the point now. 'But I will not leave until this business is over,' she added. It was good to give a promise. It would prevent her from leaving, no matter how hard it might become.

'There is no reason why you should stay for this,' Rowena said quietly. Even with the stress, she had not lost the music in her voice, but she could not make the effort to smile.

Mariah gave a little grunt, unaware of it until she heard her own voice in the stillness of the room. 'Shall we consider that all the politenesses have been offered, and reach the point? Cullen was not a perfect man, but he was an extremely good one, and I don't believe he ever stooped to a lie. Perhaps most importantly, he was ours — your family and my friend. This piece of vermin must not be allowed to soil his name. And he must not be allowed to soil yours either.' She made an effort to put a lift in her voice. 'He did not expect a fight, but he most certainly will get one. We have nothing left to lose, except our honour, if we do not try.'

Rowena blushed and her eyes filled with tears.

'My memories . . . '

'He is not going to take your memories!' Mariah said tartly. 'Unless you let him! What he will take is Cullen's good name in this village, which was his home. And he'll take yours, too. You don't need to be ashamed to show your face in the streets of your own village.' Her anger was evident now in the tone, the bite to it, the edge.

Rowena shuddered. 'I'm not a fighter like you, Mariah . . . '

'You don't have to be like me,' Mariah rejoined. 'I think one of me is probably more than sufficient for most people. We will fight in an orderly manner, with intelligence and strength of will.' She was telling herself, and Peter, equally as much as she was telling Rowena.

Rowena looked away. 'I don't know what we can do. We cannot stop the man from trying to clear his name . . . and . . . ' She tailed off into silence again.

'And you are frightened of him,' Mariah finished for her, but gently, not with the sting of contempt she might have had even a year ago.

Peter looked at her with pain in his face.

Rowena turned away so only her profile was visible, a tear sliding down her cheek.

It was time for the truth, Mariah's own truth. She could not expect Rowena to face the terror inside her if she believed Mariah held her in contempt, and had no understanding of her pain. Even this morning she had not thought it possible to speak out, but now she saw that to speak a little of it, but not of the darkest secrets

44

— never those! — was the only course of action. She took a deep breath.

'I know what it is to be frightened,' she said quietly. She even considered reaching out to touch Rowena's hand on the flowered coverlet, but that was too far outside the character she had always shown.

Of course Rowena did not believe her. Neither did Peter.

Mariah clenched her own hands, below the level of the bed, where no one else could see them. It must be done.

'I was terrified of my husband,' she said very quietly, avoiding looking at Rowena. 'And too ashamed even to tell anyone at all. I lived with it all my married life. The only time I ever fought back, he beat me so hard I never did it again. I allowed him to destroy everything in me that was good.'

Rowena was too stunned to speak.

It was Peter who interrupted her.

'Much, perhaps,' he said softly. 'But certainly not everything. And you will help us beat Owen Durward.' He hesitated. 'Would it be too melodramatic to say that you have been to the edge and looked over? You will help us from falling in.'

Ridiculously, Mariah felt tears sting her own eyes. She really must pull herself together!

She could not answer him, or look into his face. The young man was robbing her of the cast-iron temper that had protected her from pity all her life.

'We must assemble our facts, and consider

45

what needs to be done,' she said as calmly as she could. 'Durward was charged and went to trial, so there must have been considerable evidence against him. Why was he ever suspected?' She turned to Rowena. 'I don't suppose Cullen told you any details, but you must have been aware of at least some of the evidence. It happened here in the village. Neither Peter nor I were here at the time, but you were. What do you know?'

'I . . . I can't really remember,' Rowena said hesitantly.

Peter cut in before Mariah could. 'You can try, Grandmother,' he urged. 'We have to do this. The girl's name was Christina Abbott. Her father was an architect. She was fourteen at that time.'

'We all know that,' Rowena said hopelessly. 'She disappeared late one afternoon. She had been doing some homework and when she finished it, she went to visit a friend. Mary . . . something. Mary Wade! She never got there.'

'Where was her house, and where was Mary Wade's house?' Mariah asked. If Rowena gave her the street names, she could still picture the village clearly enough to imagine which way the girl had walked.

'Christina lived on Woodend Road to the west, and Mary about two doors beyond the church, to the east,' Rowena replied.

Mariah thought for a moment. 'Then she would have passed through the middle of the village, and passed your house here, and then the doctor's surgery and his house on the west side, before getting to Mary's house, or the

46

church. How far did she get? Someone must have seen her!'

'No one saw her after she passed here,' Rowena said quietly. 'We are half a mile from the church, or less.'

'Why was Durward suspected?' Mariah persisted. 'We can look it up, if we have to, but it would be difficult. Think back. The investigation happened here. There must have been questions. Talk?'

Rowena thought for a moment. 'She knew him,' she said slowly. 'He was her doctor, of course. And she was ill every now and then, as everyone is.'

'Was she pretty?' Mariah asked. 'Friendly? Would she have trusted him?'

'I think we . . . we all did.' Rowena frowned, trying to recall. 'He was the village doctor, after all. And, yes . . . ' her voice grew a little unsteady. 'She was pretty. I suppose most young girls are, in their own way, but she was prettier than most. She was graceful . . . she had beautiful hair . . . ' She tailed off into silence.

'Was Durward the only doctor?' Mariah pressed.

'After old Dr McVeigh retired, yes, he was. Only for a while. But at that time, yes.'

'Didn't her mother go with her to the doctor's?'

'Yes, but if she met him in the street, for example, she would trust him.' Rowena's voice was full of pain, and regret. 'Christina was not a foolish girl. She would not have trusted just anyone.'

47

'Grandmother, how long was she missing?' Peter asked. 'And where did they find her?' Now his voice was rough-edged too. It was clear that he found it difficult to ask.

Rowena closed her eyes and her hand on the bedclothes fumbled as she tried to grasp on to something, then she knotted her fingers around a piece of the quilt.

Mariah wondered whether to touch her or not. Perhaps she should not interrupt?

'She was gone nearly a week before they found her,' Rowena answered in a voice tight with tension, almost hoarse. 'In the copse of trees up by Benson's farm. The police said she had been horribly violated, that she must have been dead most of that time. Four or five days, at the very least.'

Peter sat silently.

Even Mariah could think of nothing to say for several moments. She tried to imagine it, and felt rage and pity choke her. She could not bear to think of it, and yet she must. Only pain was sharp enough to drive her forward.

'Somebody did that to her!' Mariah responded, the emotion in her voice unmistakable. She had no power to disguise it. 'Either Durward, or someone else. Whoever it was, he has never been caught. He is still out there, and who knows what he is doing now?'

'Don't say that!' Rowena shouted, suddenly strident.

'Of course, another culprit could be dead by now,' Mariah went on. 'But Durward isn't. He's very much alive. Do you want him living back here in Haslemere?'

'Don't say that!' This time it was a whisper.

'Whether I say it or not, it's still true.' Mariah knew the matter had to be settled now, or it would remain with them all their lives. 'We stop him here, or not at all.' She turned to Peter. 'There must have been a reason the police arrested Durward and charged him. Have we found out any of that? Someone saw him near there, or he said something that was suspicious? Someone saw him with her? He had blood on his clothes? Scars or scratches he couldn't account for? They wouldn't arrest the local doctor without a very good cause.'

Peter looked uncomfortable. 'I did ask. I knew it would come up when some wretched reporter tracked me down; knew my name was Peter Wesley. I only found what was given in evidence at the trial, and of course it was all argued, contested, thrown into doubt. It had to have been, because he got off.'

'Well, tell us anything you heard!' Mariah demanded. 'We need to know what was said, and how it was ruled out, or explained away.'

Peter looked at Rowena. 'I'll tell you downstairs. Grandmother doesn't have to hear this.'

Mariah did not move. 'Yes, she does. She may know if it was true or not. And she may know how Cullen planned to get around it.' She looked at Rowena. 'When Cullen took on the case, did he believe Durward was innocent?'

Rowena's face was white. 'I'm not certain,' she hesitated. 'He told us he believed the evidence

49

was all circumstantial, whatever that means, but he certainly believed Durward should be defended honestly, and with all the skill he could bring to it. It was a very terrible crime . . . ' She closed her eyes. 'He could not tell me the details, but he said that if Durward were found guilty, he would unquestionably be hanged.' She gulped and swallowed. 'He felt very strongly that one . . . that all of us . . . must be absolutely certain the charge, in all its details, was correct. He said it was better that a guilty man should go free than that an innocent man should be hanged. I argued with him. I think it was because I knew Christina, and her family.' She raised her hand from the quilt, and then dropped it again. 'I know that isn't reasonable, or fair, and he told me that had nothing to do with it.' She looked at Mariah. 'You knew Cullen. Do you think that made him all the more determined to defend Durward, because I could not have? I . . . I suppose I wanted him got rid of. I wanted Cullen to refuse to represent him!'

Mariah knew what Rowena meant. Cullen would do it on principle. He would have stood up for the person no one else would defend. Rowena knew it too, which was why she was now asking.

'No, Grandmother,' Peter said, looking from one to the other of them. 'You mustn't blame yourself.'

'Peter is right,' Mariah replied. 'He might have thought the scales were tipped unfairly against Durward. Once you've hanged a man, it doesn't matter how sorry you are, or how deeply you acknowledge your mistake, if there was one, you can't get him back. I know he didn't like hanging anyway, but this was a capital case . . . ' As she said it, the memories flooded her mind of their discussion. It had been here, in this house, in the sitting room downstairs. Rowena had gone to bed. Mariah and Cullen had remained, talking by the fireside. It was winter, like this, and it was cold and dark beyond the richly curtained windows.

They had talked about law, and justice, and the differences between them, about mistakes, honest or not, and miscarriages of justice that had ruined lives. She could hear his voice in her mind, and see his face in the firelight, so alive with the passion of his beliefs. He was a beautiful man, not in the outward sense of perfect features, but inwardly, with his compassion, his intense love of fairness, his delight in loveliness of every sort, from the logic of mathematics to the touch of a kitten's body as it purred, or the sound of a violin in the hands of a master.

If Durward had killed Cullen, would Mariah be happy to see him hanged for it? That was a subject she could not face at the moment. Thank God it was not her choice. She could be a detective, passionate to uncover the truth, and prove it — but never a juror.

But if Durward were here, bent on ruining Cullen's reputation, or that of Rowena, the wife whom Cullen had loved, then Mariah would fight against Durward with whatever weapons her hand could grasp.

'And do we know why he refused to continue

51

the case?' Peter said softly, looking first at Rowena, then at Mariah.

'No,' Rowena replied. 'I asked him. But he refused to speak of it. He said it would be unethical for him.'

'Could it have been personal?' Peter could not yet let it go.

'Cullen? No, never!' Rowena said fiercely, a flush of pink up her cheeks. 'He defended many people he did not like at all. Sometimes they were guilty, but there were circumstances that made it less terrible than it looked. He always said that he was their advocate, never their judge.'

Mariah could remember that, too. Another conversation by the fire. He had told her, with some self-deprecation, of a case he had defended when he was much younger, convinced the man was guilty. His mentor at the time, when he was quite junior in his law firm, had told him to defend the man with all his skills. It was an order. Cullen had done so, reluctantly, only to discover in the end that the man was actually innocent — dislikeable, but innocent of that particular crime. They had laughed about it together, he and Mariah. She remembered it for the moment of ease, but also because she herself had been misjudged because of her temper, her unkindness in the most bitter of her married years. If she had been charged with cruelty, she would have hated Cullen to know it, but she could not have asked for a better advocate to find the good in her, and speak for that.

Now she was aware that Peter was watching her.

'He had a reason,' she said, as if the matter were now beyond contesting. 'A good reason why he couldn't go on. I think we need to find out what that was, if we possibly can. It must almost certainly have something to do with what happened afterwards, and why Durward has come back.'

'Are we sure Durward was guilty?' Peter asked.

Mariah looked at his face. In that moment he seemed far younger than his thirty years. She could see the boy in him, in the days after Cullen's death. She would like to have protected him from doubt, from discovery of the small things he would rather not have known, and yet now it was inevitable. That was another reason to hate Owen Durward! If he was guilty?

'I believe so,' she told Peter. 'But of course I don't know.'

He smiled uncertainly, but he did not say anything.

⋆ ⋆ ⋆

Mariah gained Rowena's permission, and spent almost all the rest of the day in Cullen's study, which was, even after all these years, still much as he had left it. His books and papers were dusted every week by the housemaid, and nothing had been taken away. Were they kept for any reason?

Or was it just that Rowena had never found the heart to give them away, or to destroy

53

anything? Had part of her feared this day would come, and the whole issue would be opened up again?

Mariah thought not.

To begin with, she was dismayed. There was so much. Then it occurred to her that perhaps the papers were kept in either order of subject, or more likely, order of occurrence. What she needed would be from the last month or so of his life. If she started at the latest file, and worked backwards, she should find whatever notes he had made. They might not tell it all, but at least she would find whatever there was.

It drew her in immediately. Most papers were typed, which made the notations in his own hand easily visible. They could have been made yesterday, except there were no usable pens on his desk, and no ink in the well. It had been twenty years, but in all other ways it was as if he had been here yesterday. It was an illusion that he would ever return.

There were footsteps in the hall and for an instant Mariah was afraid Cullen would come in and ask her why she had intruded into his office. He would expect an explanation. He knew her intelligence and would not think she had read these things mistakenly. When the footsteps receded, she relaxed, but with a wave of loneliness.

She turned her attention back to the papers. They were mostly letters of business, advice in certain affairs. The files of his clients' matters had all been passed to whomever was chosen to deal with them after his death. What was left were his own diaries, comments, intentions he had not lived to fulfil. What could she learn from them? Where had he been, where had he intended to go?

It was intrusive. Some of his notes had not been intended for others to read. It was the notes on scraps of paper that were most revealing. There was a dry humour to them that brought him back to her memory so sharply the grief was re-created again, like tearing the scab off an old wound you thought was healed, to find it could still bleed. Underneath his good manners, he had been a far sharper observer of other people's foibles and vulnerabilities than even Rowena had expressed.

There were notes in his diary that Mariah was increasingly aware he had not meant anyone else to read. But she did not realise which they were until she had already read them. Going back to the arrest of Durward and Cullen's first meeting with him as a client, it was clear that Cullen did not like the man. It was there in his notes to himself, reminders to be fair, that he was the advocate, and not the judge. He chided himself for his instinctive feelings. There were comments such as 'I fear I allowed him to sense my dislike' and: 'What an arrogant fool the man is!' 'Is it fear speaking?' 'Who else will act for him if I don't?' 'Am I making a mistake here?' 'Look into this a lot more deeply.' They seemed to be written after meetings with someone whose name was illegible.

There were also marks she took a while to decipher. For example, the skull and crossbones that appeared next to points where he considered himself to have been wrong. They revealed his emotions more than he would ever have allowed anyone else to see. Possibly Rowena, but Mariah believed not.

Then the day before his death, he had written 'Oh God!' and later on the page, 'Now what? Really, I am a fool! And it's my own fault. I must deal with it.'

This was what she was looking for, and no matter how often she read it, all it conveyed to her was his distress, not any detail at all as to what it was, except possibly to do with Durward. It could be twisted to mean almost anything, and a clever lawyer would do that.

She closed the diary and put it back where she had found it, along with the letters and scraps of notes on this or that, old railway timetables, an almanac and an advertisement for a raincoat.

Even if they looked into it further, what would they find? There would be things that would hurt. Weaknesses, misjudgements. Everyone had moments they preferred to forget, errors that reflected sides of their character perhaps conquered since.

Rowena had adored Cullen. But had she known the real man? How much of his passion, his anger or his wit had he kept from her?

And Peter? His own father had died when he was very young indeed. Cullen had been the man he most admired, at least up to the age of ten, when Mariah had known him. How much truth did he want?

Then Mariah was impatient with herself. For

heaven's sake! What would either of them think of her if they knew her very deepest secrets? Rowena could not possibly understand a woman who would submit to what Mariah's husband had demanded of her! She would think Mariah filthy, depraved that she had lived through it, and stayed with him. Mariah could have told her there was no choice: in those days, a woman was her husband's property to do with as he wished. It was not rape, no matter what form it took.

She had told no one. Not ever. The humiliation was beyond words. And who on earth would believe her? If she had told anyone at all, he would have had her committed to an asylum. They would have said she was depraved, as they had said of other women who tried to fight back. She knew all of this now, and yet, fifty years after the events, she still despised herself that she had not fought back.

What would Peter think of her? That was something she could not allow into her mind. Even the idea of it was unbearable. He certainly would not see her as the person who could fight to defend his grandmother from an accusation, or to defend Cullen's name from whatever vile thing Durward would say of him. Would Peter see that Mariah was a coward? She had even lied, when she was a widow, and praised her dead husband as if he had been the sort of man she wished he had been: a man like Cullen Wesley.

Everyone had their secrets, their mistakes that should be allowed to lie buried in the past, forgotten and forgiven.

There was a knock on the door. She closed the desk before she answered.

The maid came in to say that dinner was served.

'Thank you,' Mariah replied. 'I will go upstairs and tidy myself, and be at the table in ten minutes.'

★   ★   ★

Dinner was a vaguely uncomfortable meal. The food was excellent, but they were all aware of the purpose for their being together, and it seemed artificial to speak lightly, as if Christmas were to be a celebration and there were no shadows over everything.

It was Mariah who finally shattered the presence, over a particularly delicious apple pie served with cream.

'I looked in Cullen's study,' she said in the silence. 'I found a few places to begin. He discovered something. He noted it, but only his own reaction . . . '

Rowena dropped her spoon. The silver clattered heavily on the porcelain of her plate.

'I'm sure . . . ' she murmured, picking it up again, although she did not eat any more. She never completed the sentence. Perhaps she had nothing in mind to say anyway.

'I think we need to know what it was, if we can,' Mariah continued. 'Because it was the day before he died. He wrote that he would have to do something about it, but not more than that.'

'To do with Durward?' Peter said quickly. 'He

58

discovered something that changed his mind about defending him!'

Rowena seemed frozen.

'What could that be?' Mariah asked. There was no possibility of retreat now. How deeply was she going to regret this?

Peter was considering, his face set in concentration.

'Let me think logically,' he said at last. 'Grandfather was a lawyer. He defended many people, and of course most of them were to some degree or another guilty . . . ' Rowena turned to him indignantly, about to deny it.

He put his hand on her wrist. 'Grandmother, the police are wrong sometimes, but much more often they are right. He spoke for his clients to give whatever reasons excused them to a degree. A lighter sentence, and sometimes other circumstances to take into account. He certainly didn't imagine they were all wrongly accused. Even guilty people need to have someone stand up for them!'

'Yes . . . I . . . I suppose you are right,' Rowena conceded, but there was still anger in her eyes. 'He was not very judging of people. I mean he . . . I don't know what I mean. He was a good man! But he was certainly not foolish.'

Mariah tried to sound gentle. 'It seems from what he wrote in his notes I saw that he had somehow made an error in his estimation of Durward's case. There is no mention of what it was.' She turned to Peter. 'What reasons would cause an advocate to drop a case when he was already committed to it? As we have agreed,

59

many of his clients were guilty. And clearly he knew that Durward was charged with the rape and murder of Christina Abbott.'

Peter bit his lip. 'You have the crux of it there, Mrs Ellison. Grandfather knew the charge, and obviously the possibility that the man was guilty. I don't know what else he could have discovered that would change his mind. I suppose Durward could have told him something else that he did not know, but I doubt it. Even now, Durward is still saying that he was innocent.'

Mariah could think of nothing that answered the question. They finished their dessert in silence.

Rowena excused herself early and retired to bed, asking Mariah if she would be good enough to bring her up a cup of hot milk.

Mariah fetched it from the kitchen and took it upstairs. She had a strong feeling that Rowena wanted to confide something to her that she did not wish Peter to hear.

Mariah did not really want to know it either. There were too many matters that should remain unspoken. Everyone needed privacy for old wounds, old mistakes, weaknesses that others did not need to know. Disillusion was extraordinarily painful.

She knocked on the bedroom door, and when she heard Rowena's voice, she went in.

Rowena was sitting up in bed, her hair tied loosely, her face almost ashen.

Mariah knew that it was inevitable now. She was going to learn something she would very much rather not know. Could she face it, if

Rowena broke her dream of Cullen, the man she had believed him to be? Had she idealised him, because she was dreadfully aware he would never be more than a dear friend, one whom she would rarely see, and — immensely worse, like ice around the heart — one who saw only a very little of the truth about him. And what would Cullen have thought of her, if he had known?

We all need privacy, time to repent, and to forget! Room to change, space and forgiveness so we can heal. Now they were digging into Cullen's papers to understand so they could defend him against Durward.

Or was it against an old mistake of his own, and Durward was innocent?

You don't love people because they are perfect, or were, in your mind. You love them because . . . no, because, you just do! Perhaps it is that they gave you something of love, something of being cared about, the feeling that you too were valuable to them. A gentleness, perhaps, a safety of dreams.

'What is it you want to tell me?' she said to Rowena. 'You can't drink the milk yet. It's too hot. Put it down and tell me.'

Rowena put the milk down. She had not really wanted it anyway. It was a way of getting Mariah up here, where they were alone. They both knew that.

'I made a mistake,' Rowena said softly. 'I know you thought the world of Cullen. And you were right. He was a wonderful man . . . but he could be distant at times, impatient when I didn't understand some of the things he said . . .'

Mariah did not interrupt. She could easily believe that was true. Rowena was gentle, funny, generous, but she had not been brought up to have an enquiring mind. And she had not Mariah's edge of temper to develop it for herself. Cullen had loved her, and she had made him happy in many ways. But he engaged Mariah's sharper intelligence, and her willingness to argue a point, take it apart and rethink it.

Rowena was watching her. How much did she understand?

'Owen Durward flattered me,' Rowena said quietly, avoiding Mariah's eyes now. 'Cullen knew I loved him, and would never even think of anyone else. He . . . took me for granted in . . . in some ways.'

Mariah felt a prickle of discomfort, but she did her best to deny it, even to herself.

'I allowed Durward to flirt with me,' Rowena went on, her voice growing even quieter. 'On one occasion it . . . it went too far . . . '

'What?' The moment the exclamation was out, Mariah regretted it, but it was too late.

'Not that far!' Rowena said instantly. 'Really, Mariah! I . . . I let him kiss me.' Her face was scarlet now. 'And then I pushed him away. He was . . . angry. I don't know what he imagined. He told me . . . ' She took a deep breath, struggling to continue. 'He told me that if I did not treat him with warmth in the future, he would tell Cullen, and anyone else who asked, that I had thrown myself at him, and he had been embarrassed, and . . . and revolted . . . and he had rejected me somewhat fiercely. And my dislike of him was based upon that. I didn't dare be anything but cordial to him after that. I was so ashamed. You cannot imagine . . . '

'Yes,' Mariah said immediately. 'Yes, I can imagine . . . ' She did something completely out of her character. She put her hand gently over Rowena's, and held it. 'I can imagine very well. I am so sorry such a thing happened to you. It seems that Owen Durward is a thoroughly vile man. We will not beat him easily. But we will beat him!' She had no idea if that was true or not, but she refused even to imagine failure.

★   ★   ★

Mariah had tried not to think of newspaper reporters and the damage they might inflict, but the next morning she was up early, unable to sleep, and had barely finished breakfast when the first one knocked on the door.

The footman arrived to say that a Mr Roberts, from the newspapers, wished to speak with Mrs Wesley, but Mrs Wesley was not yet up and would Mrs Ellison be kind enough to speak to him instead?

Mariah considered a variety of brief and very blunt replies, and then realised that whatever she said, or refused to say, they were likely to print it anyway. They would write something like: 'Even Mrs Wesley's closest friends refuse to explain anything, or to defend her. Mrs Mariah Ellison, who was present at the time of the original trial, and of Mr Wesley's death, will say nothing in defence of her friend.' She could not say that was untrue. And how would that look?

Reluctantly, she told the footman to let the man in. She would see him when she had finished her breakfast.

'Shall I offer him tea, ma'am?' he asked.

'Certainly not!' Mariah said tartly. 'He is not a friend; he is a nuisance that unfortunately we cannot afford to ignore. I will attend to him when I am ready. Let him wait in the morning room, where there is nothing he can meddle with or snoop into.'

'Yes, Mrs Ellison.'

Mariah finished her tea and poured a second cup, then did not want it after all. She was much more nervous about speaking to the newspaper reporter than she cared to acknowledge. Best to get it over with. Doubtless there would be more as the issue became more public.

He was a young man with unusually straight hair. It poked out at the sides, instead of curving with his head. He was pacing around the room, staring at the bookshelves when Mariah entered.

'You may sit down,' she told him coolly. 'I am Mrs Ellison, a friend of Mrs Wesley. She is not well enough to be harassed by you, or your fellows. What is it you wish to know?'

'Good morning, Mrs Ellison,' he replied, remaining on his feet. 'This is a very nice house. Mrs Wesley must be well situated to afford it.'

She raised her eyebrows. 'If that is a question to which you think I know the answer then you are mistaken. I do not enquire into the financial affairs of my friends.'

'But you know the personal affairs,' he said

with a smile. 'You knew Mr Wesley, I believe. Quite well?'

She must be careful. He phrased his questions so that a simple answer could be misunderstood. 'I have known Mrs Wesley for many years,' she agreed. 'You did not come here to ask me that. It is common knowledge. The village postman could have told you so.'

'Indeed. I could get a lot of information from the village postman, or the innkeeper, or in most of the shops,' he agreed. 'But that would be gossip. I prefer to go to the source. You were here when Mr Wesley was killed, I believe? Were you surprised?'

'You are mistaken. I was not here.'

'My information says you were.'

She wished she were free to slap that unctuous smile from his face, but that would make a marvellous article for him. She could just imagine it. She must not give him fuel for anything. He would use it.

'I was here before,' she said coolly. 'I went home. I returned when I heard the news. Is this really a matter of public concern? I do not have the time, or the inclination, to help you gain general background to your story.'

He smiled again. 'Tell me about Mr Wesley. What sort of man was he?'

Mariah kept her temper only because she had to.

'I do not speak about my friends to newspaper reporters,' she replied without raising her voice. 'I am speaking to you at all only as a courtesy. I will answer your questions of fact. I am not

65

going to write your article for you.'

'You are afraid of saying something that is not to his credit?' Roberts observed.

She looked at him coldly. 'If you are attempting to make me lose my temper, young man, you are wasting both your time and mine. I can add nothing to the facts that you should already know. I do not know who killed Christina Abbott. I do not know what evidence the police had in the case against Dr Durward, or anyone else, nor do I know why Mr Wesley withdrew from it. I do not know anything more of Mr Wesley's death than you may read in the newspapers of the time. If the police have any knowledge now that they had not then, you will have to gain it from them. I have no idea.'

He regarded her carefully. 'You are so discreet, Mrs Ellison, it makes me wonder what you are hiding. Nothing you say is spontaneous. You have prepared well for this interview, weighing every answer. You pique my curiosity. What are you hiding?'

She felt the heat rise up her face. She was quite aware that he was deliberately provoking her, and yet she had to stop herself from snapping back at him. He would use her words against her, or against Cullen, or Rowena.

She forced herself to smile, although she felt it was more a baring of her teeth.

'I do not know the answers. I must think carefully before I speak to you, in case I accidentally misinform you . . . through lack of care rather than intent to deceive. Would you prefer me to speak rashly? Surely your duty to your readers is to write what is true?'

If he detected any sarcasm in her, he did not show it.

He began again, with more questions about Rowena. They were phrased as concern, but they were intrusive, even prurient. It was a foretaste of what might be to come. She was glad Rowena was not up, and willing to answer them herself. She would have been embarrassed, even mortified by some of them. He would have twisted her emotion, and the unintended tears into remorse, or worse, fear.

Finally, she did lose her temper.

'Does your mother know what you do?' she said tartly, her eyebrows raised. 'And how you do it?'

He looked startled.

'That would make an interesting article, don't you think?' she went on. 'How does a woman face her neighbours, her friends, should she have any, and explain how her son twists the words of the frightened and bereaved, so as to make them seem dirty? Tell me, do you ever question and pursue anyone who has the ability to fight back at you? Pursue those you love? Do you have a wife? Children? Are they proud of you? Or afraid?'

'Really, Mrs Ellison — ' he protested.

She rose to her feet, lifting her weight a little by leaning on the arms of the chair. 'Of course you don't!' she answered her own question. 'If you did, you would leave them open to retaliation, and you wouldn't be so foolish. Now

67

that I have told you what little I know, you can share it with . . . what is the collective noun for journalists? A pack? You are less like hunters, more like carrion feeders. You go after the already wounded — or dead. I know it is a 'murder' of crows. That seems appropriate.' She glared at him, and was satisfied to see the colour rise in his face. 'I shall have the footman show you out.'

Peter was waiting for her in the sitting room. 'Are you all right?' he asked with some concern. 'They can be pretty . . . harsh . . . ' He rose to his feet and went to her, as if he would guide her to a chair.

'So can I!' she said more sharply than she had meant to. She would not like Peter to have seen her temper. He knew her only as she had been in this house, where she cared for the people who lived here. She would like him to keep that opinion of her. She disliked admitting it, but she cared very much what he thought of her, and not only because he reminded her of Cullen, but for himself. She would dearly have liked a son, or a grandson, like him.

She sat down, without his assistance, suddenly tired. She did not realise how tense she had been, how afraid of making an error.

The footman came almost immediately. He looked pleased with himself. He even smiled at her. Had he been listening at the door?

'The young man has gone, Mrs Ellison,' he said with satisfaction.

Mariah felt a faint heat in her cheeks. 'Were you listening?' she asked.

He remained perfectly calm. 'I remained near the door, ma'am, in case he should give you any trouble ... or you might ... wish for something.'

She changed her mind completely. 'Thank you. That was most considerate of you,' she said gravely. It was perfectly ridiculous, of course, but she liked having his approval, and his loyalty.

★ ★ ★

She spent the afternoon with Peter and, for a short time, Rowena also.

'If not Durward — and we need to consider that possibility — ' she began unhappily, ignoring Rowena's dismay, 'then who? Cullen believed he could defend Durward. Could he have done that without any other possibility being suggested?' She looked towards Rowena.

'He didn't discuss that sort of thing with me,' she said miserably. 'But he did believe he could succeed. He told me that.'

'Then either he had an idea of proving Durward innocent, for which he would have to show him to be somewhere else, or that he did not have the ability, the weapon, or whatever was used,' Mariah reasoned, turning to Peter for assurance. 'Or else he had another equally believable person to suspect.'

'How does that help?' Rowena asked.

'Because it changed,' Mariah replied. 'Something changed so Cullen could not defend him any longer.'

Rowena's face was almost without colour at

all. 'I told you, Mariah! Durward must have told him about my . . . my misjudgement!' She sounded desperate and she looked away from Peter, as if he would read the whole story in her face.

Peter looked at Mariah, too, the question unmistakable in his eyes.

How much truth was necessary? Once told it could never be untold again.

'You are making too much of it,' Mariah said dismissively. 'You were embarrassed because he misunderstood, or pretended to: He would not be so stupid as to risk losing the best lawyer in the county over such a trifle. Nor would Cullen have believed it for a moment. Really, Rowena! Was Cullen that kind of man?'

'No . . . but . . . ' Rowena did not know how to finish. She stared miserably towards the window, and the bare garden, branches stark against a grey sky.

Mariah turned to Peter. 'Cullen believed Durward was innocent and was willing to defend him rather than try to plead insanity, which would be about the only excuse for such a monstrous crime. Then he changed his mind. We must find out what happened, and perhaps from that we can deduce something useful. We need to know what he believed to begin with, and find the fact that changed it.'

'How on earth can we do that?' Rowena said wearily. 'All his papers relating to the case went to the lawyer who took over from him. I can't even remember his name now. Anyway, he died several years ago. He wasn't a young man. And he got Durward off! Even if he was guilty, and we could prove it, which we can't, what good would it do now?'

Mariah felt disheartened herself. What good would it do, indeed?

'It would prove that Grandfather left the case for a good reason!' Peter said, but there was a note of despair in his voice too. 'And it had nothing to do with you.' He looked at Rowena, then reached over and put his hand on her arm. 'Grandmother, Durward is suggesting that you had something to do with Grandfather's death, because he discovered something about you that he couldn't live with. Something that Durward told him, and he believed it. I'm sorry you have to hear it. I would have kept it from you if I could, but that's what the newspapers are digging for. And sooner or later, some wretched person in the village is going to say enough to feed the gossip.'

Her voice was a whisper. 'I've heard it already, my dear. Cullen knew all sorts of things about people, because he was their lawyer. They imagine I knew them too, but they're quite wrong. He never told me anything. He was an honourable man! He was nothing like what they are suggesting. It's . . . vile!'

'Then we must fight,' Peter replied. 'Mustn't we, Mariah?'

It was a challenge, and the first time he had called her directly by her name. Perhaps it was an impertinence from a man his age, or perhaps it was an affection, as if they were somehow related.

71

'We must,' she agreed. 'And we will begin by going to see Owen Durward. Peter, you will find out where he is staying and arrange for us to call upon him. By 'us' I mean you and me. Rowena will stay here, and definitely not speak to anyone who might call. You are ill, do you understand? We cannot afford to be misquoted, or forced to defend anything until we have the weapons with which to do it.'

'Yes, Mariah,' Rowena said wearily. 'I have no wish to speak to anyone.'

'You can look at Cullen's diaries and papers and see if you can find any reference to Durward, or Christina, or anything else that may be helpful. I shall sort them out while Peter is making our arrangements.' It was not a question; it was an order.

Rowena did not reply, but neither did she argue.

★   ★   ★

Mariah and Peter went together to see Owen Durward late in the afternoon. At this time of the year, just a few days before Christmas, it was dark by four o'clock, especially on a grey and windy day with rain threatening. Walking was not a pleasure, but with no luggage to carry, it was not far. They walked in companionable silence. There was nothing further to discuss, and neither of them felt like making conversation. Their footsteps on the pavement were the only sounds.

Mariah was horribly aware of how close they

were to complete failure, and she did not want to say anything that would allow her mood to darken Peter's spirits even further. He had turned to her for help and she was failing him.

Durward was staying at the inn, but he had taken a large sitting room as well as a bedroom, which afforded him privacy where he could receive whomever he chose.

He answered the door of his room, looking first at Peter, barely noticing Mariah. He was a tall man, striking in appearance with thick iron-grey hair and a face that might have been handsome, were it a little less predatory.

'Good afternoon, Wesley,' he said with a very slight twist of humour. 'I'm not at all sure what I can do for you, but as I recall, you were a child when we last met, and this whole wretched affair began. So you are hardly to blame for any of it. Come in.' He stepped aside to allow Peter to pass.

Then his eye fell on Mariah. 'Mrs Ellison! What a pleasant surprise that you are still with us. Please come in also.' His expression was impossible to read. He was perhaps twenty years younger than she, but he managed to make it sound like several generations.

She went in and sat down without comment. She had not expected courtesy from him. That he received them at all was sufficient.

'What can I do for you, Mr Wesley?' Durward asked, still speaking only to Peter. 'If you have come to apologise, it is misplaced. You had no part in the matter.' He lifted one shoulder very slightly. It was a curiously dismissive gesture. 'If, on the other hand, you have come to ask me not to try to reinstate my reputation, you must surely realise that your journey is pointless. I want to return to Haslemere, and I cannot do that until I have demonstrated not only that the law has no claim on me, but that I was wrongly accused in the first place. To do that, I imagine you appreciate that I have no need to prove I was innocent of Christina's death, but that Cullen Wesley's death resulted from his own unfortunate domestic affairs, and was in no way my fault. I have lived under this shadow for twenty years. I will not do so any longer.'

Peter drew in his breath, but it was Mariah who spoke.

'Why now, Mr Durward? Why, after all this time, rake up the matter again?'

He turned to her, his eyebrows raised, his voice edged with irritation. 'Your question is pointless, madam. I choose to. If you think a plea that so much time has elapsed will deter me, you are more of a fool than I had thought.'

'I was not looking for mercy!' Mariah snapped. 'I was curious. It is a dangerous thing you are doing. For you, as well as for others. You must have a reason. Something to gain?' She emphasised the last word with the same ugly edge to her voice as he had used.

He was surprised. It was clear in the momentary hesitation in his face. 'You are quite right. There is no reason to hide it. I am going to marry a woman of good family, and standing. A widow. I cannot expect her to live under this shadow of . . . unpleasantness.'

'A widow with money, no doubt,' Mariah responded.

Durward shot her a look that, for a moment, frightened her. Then his face smoothed out into a smile. 'She is also charming, Mrs Ellison, of a gentle nature and great kindness. Such qualities are rare.' His implication against her inclusion was clear.

'In your acquaintance, perhaps,' she said instantly. 'I can see that you do not wish her to perceive such a cloud hanging over your head. But since you have already been tried and found to be not guilty, surely the case is settled. You do not need to live here in Haslemere, where the matter will always be of some pain.'

'Certainly I have been proven not guilty of the girl's death,' he agreed. 'But you are missing the point. Cullen Wesley was also killed and violently, Mrs Ellison. No one believed the fiction that he overbalanced the bookcase on himself, and the idiotic ornamental cannonball struck him on the head as the whole thing collapsed. He, too, was killed! Murdered, if you insist on the word. No one was charged with that.' There was anger in his face now, completely undisguised, as was the malice.

'I see.' The ice inside her was painful, like an old terror brought back complete. She had seen that same look in her husband's eyes, before he had struck her, or worse. She had never stood up to him, but now was her chance to defend herself at last. She would not be a coward this time, whatever the cost to her.

'And you are afraid that you will be charged?'

she said with a very slight smile. He would never know that her stomach was churning and she could hardly breathe. 'I understand. It is a very reasonable fear. He had suddenly withdrawn from defending you. We would assume it was because he had discovered something about you that was indefensible. So you had to be certain he would remain silent. His word was not enough. To a man who had no honour himself, it was unimaginable to you that he would keep his word.' She took a shallow breath. She must say it all now; she might never have another chance. 'Were you afraid he would blackmail you for the rest of your life?'

The silence in the room seemed to throb, like a living thing.

Peter stared at her, struggling to grasp what she had said.

Slowly Durward's face changed, an ugly, mottled colour coming to his cheeks.

'Blackmail? How like a woman. I see now why you are Mrs Wesley's friend. You were here then, weren't you! Plain, dumpy, ill-tempered Mrs Ellison seemed such an unlikely friend for the pretty, unsatisfied Mrs Wesley. But you were her confidante, her acolyte, living your own frustrated dreams through her!'

Peter half rose in his chair, his face white. 'Mrs Ellison has been our family's friend through good times and bad!' he said furiously, his voice low and very clear. 'Yes, she is bad-tempered, but she's brave and she's clever, and she's loyal. You are none of these things. All you can do is seek to destroy those who are better than you are.'

'Sit down, you fool!' Durward raised his voice, then calmed it again. 'You know nothing. You think your grandfather was some kind of saint? He was a weak man strutting around the stage of a small town, playing at being a lawyer.' He leaned forward a little, ignoring Mariah now, all his malice bent upon Peter. 'Your grandmother was a pretty woman, not beautiful, but pleasing in an empty way. He couldn't satisfy anything in her, not her hunger and not her dreams. She threw herself at me. It was pathetic, and in its way, revolting.' He relished the word, licking his lips as if he meant to repeat it. 'I rejected her. I had to! Neither of them ever forgave me for it. She was humiliated. He felt insulted beyond bearing. His wife had offered herself to another man, and been turned down. He couldn't live with it.'

'You are saying he hit his own head with a cannon-ball?' Mariah said incredulously. 'Little wonder you are afraid no one will believe you.'

'How did he even know about it?' Peter asked, returning to his chair, almost as if Durward had ceased to be a threat except in his own imagination.

Mariah stared at Durward. 'You told him!' she accused. 'Why? And why in heaven's name would he believe you?' She looked him up and down as if he were repulsive. In her own mind she was looking at her husband as she should have done years ago.

'I had to!' Now he was glaring at her. 'How could I trust a man to defend me, when that secret was waiting to be revealed? In my place,

77

would you have trusted your life in the hands of a man whose wife had thrown herself at you?' He turned to Peter. 'Would you?'

Mariah saw the hurt, and the struggle in Peter's face.

She answered for him, looking straight at Durward. 'If I were someone who had never broken my word, or acted out of spite or personal revenge, then I probably would,' she said. 'On the other hand, if I were selfish, a liar, jealous of better men than I, then I would probably expect them to act the same way. A thief thinks everyone else steals also. You explain yourself very well.' She ignored his body tensing and moving forward in his chair as if he would lunge out of it, at her. 'And even if you were guilty, he would have defended you, which is the part of it that puzzles me. At least to begin with, he intended to do that. What changed his mind, Mr Durward?'

'Dr Durward,' he corrected her sharply. 'And I have already told you that. But you are so besotted with him you refuse to believe it. He could not hold his wife's interest or affection, and when he discovered that she had offered herself, very explicitly, to me, and that I had been embarrassed and repulsed by it, he hated me with the passion, and the venom, only a weak man can have. It is not my fault that you cannot see that.' His eyes were unmoving on her face. 'But I can do all in my power to see that it is believed! Perhaps when the whole town knows it at last, then you will be obliged to accept, or appear even more ridiculous than you do now. At least, so far, you have kept your folly more or less to yourself. Do you not mind being a laughing stock? An object of pity?'

'I care what I am, Dr Durward, not what others may imagine me to be,' she snapped back. 'I don't live here. And any contempt these people may have for me is well matched by mine for them, if they turn against Mrs Wesley, whom they have known all their lives.'

'Bravo! Well said. I wonder if you will say it so bravely and with such conviction when Mrs Wesley is laughed at, and Mr Wesley's pathetic jealousy is known?' Durward leaned forward a little further, until his face was only a couple of feet away from hers. 'And when she is charged with murdering him, will she then tell us all that she did so in self-defence, because he attacked her for her . . . prostitution of herself to me? Will she thank you for threatening me into defending myself by exposing her?'

Peter rose to his feet.

'Mariah is not afraid of you, Dr Durward. She may be old, and a woman alone, but she will not give in to you, and neither will I.'

'And your grandmother?' Durward asked, also standing now. 'Do you think she will thank you for this, from whatever prison they take her to, before they hang her?'

'You are ahead of yourself.' Mariah rose awkwardly, gripping the arms of her chair to aid herself. Her muscles had been so tight that now they ached as she stood. 'If Christina had been your only victim, you could have walked away. We lost that one. But you have wakened a lot of old memories. You are a fool, Doctor! An arrogant fool.' And she marched out of the door, heavy footed and angry, but also frightened. She had taken it too far. This was not how she had intended to conduct a very awkward encounter.

Peter caught up with her in the front hall, just as she walked through the doorway out into the street.

'You were magnificent,' he said, taking her arm in spite of her attempt to pull away. She had made a bad misjudgement and she did not want excusing for it.

'You have made him really angry,' Peter went on as they crossed the street, startling the baker's horse and causing the whole vehicle to swerve. 'But I saw fear in his face also, just for a moment. It's going to be dangerous. May I call you 'Aunt Mariah'? I feel absurd calling you 'Mrs Ellison' all the time. I don't have any actual aunts. I think we had better not tell Grandmother about this. Or not all about it.'

Mariah was so startled by his suggestion that for a moment or two she was unable to think of anything to say. It was ridiculous to feel so very pleased. And she was also frightened. She knew what Durward had done to Christina. It was idiotic to pray for the past to have been different, but silently, in her head, she prayed anyway — please God, the girl had not known what he had done to her! Let it have been that she was not conscious.

'Yes,' she said. 'Of course you may call me . . . Aunt, if you care to.' She hurried on, in case he changed his mind. 'But we must tell Rowena at least some of this. She may be able to defend herself more completely than we know.' She took a breath. 'Now! We must think of any weapon we have, or can obtain, against this vile man.'

Peter tried to hide a twisted, painful smile, fighting down his fear. 'Yes, Aunt Mariah.' He took her arm more firmly and guided her along the footpath, past the gaily decorated shop windows filled with toys, sweetmeats, brightly coloured ornaments and cards. Then finally away from the lights and pavements on to the road home, merely another half-mile with the fading sunlight marking the way, and the rising wind moving the laurel leaves a little, but not strong enough yet to whine in the bare trees.

Within five minutes they could see the familiar outline of home, and the light on in the doorway.

★   ★   ★

Peter kept his word, and he told Rowena in general terms what had transpired at their meeting with Durward. Mariah was not present. She was certain that Rowena would prefer her not to be. She used the time to study such papers as she had found relating to Durward, mostly scribbled notes Cullen had written to remind himself of points to consider. As before, the tone of them conveyed to her both that Cullen had not personally liked Durward, far from it, but he had believed he'd discovered a defence. There was always the possibility that Durward was not guilty of Christina's death. No one should be condemned because they were unpleasant. Wryly, Mariah conceded that she, of all people, could not afford that!

Mariah found herself smiling as she moved from one piece of paper to another. The words brought Cullen's memory back to her as if twenty years had disappeared. She could hear his voice again, the unique timbre of it, his choice of words, and so often the humour.

She herself had been ill-tempered, perhaps even as much as Durward, if much less offensive. Her son's wife, Caroline, had put up with her. Everyone had, except on occasion one of her granddaughters. Actually she liked that one, Charlotte, the best. People are rude for many reasons, most of them rooted in one kind of unhappiness or another. It is not an excuse, but there was no way now of going back and undoing it.

What was Durward's reason? Hatred of a man he knew was better than he? Fear of losing something?

What had her reason been for her own ill temper, if she were honest? There was no need to ask twice. She despised herself for allowing her husband to use her as he had. She had been legally bound to him in a society that would not tolerate rebellion. She remembered him so clearly and could see his face again in her mind. But for the first time, she recognised that behind the cruelty was fear and self-hatred, a man who needed to inflict his inner pain outward. He hated himself, and Mariah even more, because he knew that she understood all his weakness. Now she also realised how he must have hated her because she was the one he had injured, and she was the reminder of all that he had become.

Mariah leaned forward over the desk, and put her head in her hands, letting the tears come at last. And then she pulled herself together as a new thought struck her. Could it be something in himself that Durward hated?

If he had first raped and then killed Christina Abbott, then he had every reason to loathe himself, and fear the thing within him that had caused it. He lived in a nightmare. If it were simply his own nightmare, then she would have pitied him. But as it was, she fully intended to use it against him, if she could just think how.

Peter knocked on the door and came into the study the moment she answered. He looked tired and very sad. He sat down in the other chair, his face pale, his hair flopping forward where he had run his hands through it.

'Grandmother is devastated.' His voice was quiet, catching a little in his throat. His hands on his knees were clenched, knuckles white. 'I don't know what else to say to her.'

He looked at Mariah and she was aware of all the other things for which he did not wish to find words. He was disappointed, confused that the grandmother he had loved since childhood, who had sat up with him when he was ill, told him stories, cooked his favourite foods for him herself, was now so much in need of his strength and his patience.

'She's afraid of him,' he added simply. 'And I think she's very tired of living here alone, quietly facing growing older, knowing what the people of the village think of her. Some of them have been very cruel, and now it will get worse.'

'Of course it will,' Mariah agreed. 'Because she will not come out and fight against them. It is not who she is to fight, it never was. I could remind every one of them of all the kindnesses she has offered, and the times she has helped them and listened to their griefs, without judging them, or ever repeating what she knew. If only she would face them.'

'She won't.' He shook his head. 'She misses Grandfather. It's all she can think about.'

'Of course she does.' Mariah thought how much she herself had missed Cullen Wesley, even though he was no real part of her life, only of her dreams. 'We shall have to fight for her.' She looked across the short distance that separated them. She could see Peter in her memory as a child, all the happiness taken from him in a single tragedy. He and Rowena had helped each other. For him, she had kept at least a fragment of her strength.

Now it was Mariah's turn to do that.

'I have been thinking . . . '

He looked up.

She had no intention of telling him all her thoughts, just the ones that might be useful. 'We are both quite sure that Durward is guilty, and that Rowena must have been nice to him on one occasion, and he either genuinely misunderstood, or he chose to. Cullen would have known that, and perhaps chided her, more likely made a joke of it. He would know that she was innocent of anything except misjudgement.'

'Yes,' he agreed.

'So something else caused him to change his mind about defending Durward,' she continued. 'Something far more serious than disliking the man. He did that from the start. His notes make it clear.'

Peter's eyes widened with interest. 'Why? What did he say?'

'It is not what he said, it is the words he used,' she explained. 'References perhaps no one else would understand. But they are of no use, except to guide us. We must learn all we can about Durward.'

'They found him not guilty,' he reminded her.

'Humph! And do you believe that?' she asked. 'Were they right?'

'I . . . '

'Be honest!' she pushed. 'No one else has been found guilty! Why do you think your grandfather backed out of defending him?' Before he could answer, she did so herself. 'He found out something that made it intolerable for him to get the man off. Maybe he couldn't tell anyone, but he was certain.'

'Why wouldn't he tell anyone?'

'Because he needed proof. And when he had got it, Durward killed him,' she said, as if she had no doubt.

'Aunt Mariah, I know you want to defend — ' he began, his voice gentle and sad.

'Listen to me, Peter!' She made up her mind even as she was saying the words. 'Yes, I do want to defend Rowena and Cullen, and you,' she agreed. 'And I want to catch Durward and make

85

sure he never does anything so terrible again, to a girl like Christina Abbott, or anybody else. And yes, right at the moment I would like to see him suffer. But that isn't the point. I . . . ' She saw the look on his face and wondered if she really had the courage to carry this through. She had the perfect opportunity to escape. Why didn't she just take it? It would be so much easier.

Because she had retreated all those years, for herself. Fate, or whoever was in charge of it, had given her a chance to fight back now, for someone else, perhaps someone she would never know, but if she did not take it this one time, there might never be another. She was an old woman. She was going to grasp it with both hands, even if it cut her to the bone!

She looked at him for a moment, then away again. She started to speak in a low, urgent voice.

'Whoever it was that killed Christina, he did terrible things to her first. Men who do things like that do it because they have a hunger inside them that is never fed.'

Peter drew in his breath to speak.

'Don't interrupt me!' she ordered. 'I am not speaking lightly. I've already told you and Rowena something of my own story, something I've never before told to anyone. I wish I could have lived the rest of my life without telling you, but you need to understand. Men like Durward always come back, they cannot help it. But they are never satisfied for long. Whoever killed Christina would do it again, unless he were stopped.'

This time he did not interrupt.

'I know it of Durward,' she continued. 'I can see it in his eyes. And I think perhaps he knows I see it. Both of us have tasted in the air something familiar: a knowledge of pain.' At last she looked up at him. His eyes were so gentle it startled her. He was not revolted, not angry with her for her cowardice. He believed her, but did he understand?

'It is my chance to fight this time,' she told him. 'I am not going to back away. I will do all I can to see that Rowena is not hurt, but he has scented vulnerability, and he will not stop. He wishes to marry well, financially it may even be necessary for him. Whatever the reason, he is compelled to settle this now. The cost to Rowena, or to you, is immaterial to him.'

'I'm sorry,' he said, studying her face as he spoke. His voice was gentle. 'I wish it hadn't been necessary for you to relive old wounds, or to tell anyone else about them.'

'Don't be,' she replied. 'Perhaps I should have done it long ago. We must use whatever skills or understanding we have. Cullen knew something for which Durward killed him. He had understood too much, and he could not defend him for some reason he considered beyond his ability or his duty to overlook. He found it out shortly before he was killed. Durward could not leave it and risk someone else finding out too. We need to know what Cullen did, where he went, who he spoke to in the two or three days before he died.'

'Grandmother will know.' Peter did not wait for her to argue. 'I will go and ask her. I don't think we can waste time.'

It was later in the evening, after dinner, and they were all three sitting beside the fire, curtains drawn closed, keeping out not only the darkness of the night, and much of the chill, but also the sound of the rising wind and the increasing spatter of rain. There were candles lit, rather than the gas brackets on the walls, and they gave the room a timeless, gentle light.

Rowena told them she did not know to whom Cullen had spoken regarding the case, but she said he had taken a trip on the train, and returned deeply disturbed. He had said nothing to her, beyond that he must now consider exactly what he should do.

'He spent all evening in his study,' she said very quietly. 'He did not eat any supper, and when I went to bed, he was still in there, with the light on over the desk.'

'And he never told you?' Peter pressed.

'No. There . . . there was little chance.' She blinked, and kept her composure with obvious difficulty. When she continued her voice was husky. 'He went out the next day, and I believe it was some time in the afternoon that he went to see Durward, and told him that he could not continue with the case.'

'He saw him in prison?' Mariah asked quickly.

Rowena shook her head. 'No, it was before the trial, and since the evidence against Durward was so slight, so . . . circumstantial — I think that is the word — he was on bail, confined to his house, but there was no guard to keep him there. And do not forget that he was a respected doctor, and we all thought we knew him. And, of course, he protested that he was innocent, and would prove it. Many people believed him. I think they still do. We are all inclined to trust our doctor — we need to! He relied on that. Running away would have settled his guilt. A police constable called by regularly.'

'Could he have left?' Peter asked, knowing where Mariah's thoughts were leading.

'I suppose so,' Rowena said hesitantly. 'It was dark early, but not especially cold. And there was a full moon. I was out.' Her face clouded with misery at the recollection. 'I went to get sticks for the fire . . . to light it, you know? It was a task I enjoyed. I did it most evenings. When I came home, Cullen was . . . was lying on the floor of his study, with the bookcase crashed beside him, and that . . . that wretched cannonball smeared with blood by his head.' She made a visible effort to control herself. 'I never knew what he learned, or why he could not continue to represent Durward.' She closed her eyes for a moment, as if that would shut out the memories.

'The police came, of course,' she continued after a moment. 'They were uncertain whether it was really an accident or not, but the servants had seen no one around . . . which of course they wouldn't have done. Not if they came in through the back way, or over from the street, unless somebody was out walking. And I could not prove I had been collecting sticks. I put them in the outhouse as I came back, with the others from previous days, to keep them dry. Perhaps

89

it's an eccentric thing to do?'

'Very natural,' Mariah said, although she had no idea. She lived in the city, and maids attended to the fires. Rowena chose to contribute to her own house; she was a countrywoman. She did her own gardening, apart from the digging, and she did it for pleasure and a creative mind with shape and colours. She knew the names and seasons of the flowers, and what type of soil they needed, and whether to plant them in the sun or the shade.

'The train ride,' Peter prompted. 'Where did he go?'

'He didn't tell me.'

'Then how long did he take?'

'He was gone most of the day. I . . . I really don't know.'

'Then we will have to look at the train timetables of that year and see what was available. He must have had a reason. It looks very possible that whatever he learned, it was that day.'

Mariah agreed with him. Regardless of how tedious it was, this seemed their best chance of learning whatever Cullen had discovered. Perhaps it was their only chance. Time was short. They neither of them mentioned it, but earlier they had both heard the increasingly ugly whispers in the village, some of them growing more and more open. Mariah would like to have told the gossips what she thought of them, but losing her temper now, however justifiable, would detract from the work that mattered.

Peter found a railway timetable current to

Cullen's death among the books in the study, and brought it back to the sitting room. It was the first and most obvious place to look. Unfortunately, there was no mark in it, but that was not surprising. Cullen was not a man to have defaced a book for any reason.

'See where it falls open of itself,' Mariah told him. She was too eager to be diplomatic. 'Try it a few times!' She was standing up beside him, sensing victory, even a small one. Rowena remained sitting, still not able to believe in victory. To her it was a phantom, a dream without hope. It was clear in her eyes, and the slump of her shoulders.

Peter gave her a quick glance, his eyes bright. Obediently, he let the book fall open four or five times. Twice it fell at the same place.

'Where is it?' Mariah demanded.

'The local line east and west,' he replied.

'I wish we knew what time he left.' She stared at the page with its rows of times and destinations.

'Probably one of the earlier ones,' Peter replied. 'But we don't know which way he went.'

'We shall have to try both ways, if we cannot find out.' She did not intend to be put off, not by anything at all. She did not believe for an instant that Rowena had been responsible for Cullen's death, and the only way to prove that was to find out who had. Everything else was Durward's word against hers. And since so many of the villagers had been willing to blame her, they would find it difficult now to retract, without profound apology, and a cloud of guilt hanging over them for their malice. Few people admitted to such, unless forced to.

'We could try the stationmaster,' Peter said hopefully. 'Since it was close to Christmas, and he knew Grandfather personally, he may remember that day. It was the last time they would have met.'

'An excellent idea, if it is still the same man?' Mariah agreed.

'It is,' Peter affirmed. 'I will go and see him first thing tomorrow morning. Then perhaps I can go wherever Grandfather went.'

'I shall come with you,' she said firmly.

'It's going to be cold and probably wet also. And I don't know how far it is,' he warned.

She gave him a withering look that he should even think of refusing her. She had no intention of being left behind, and he should have known that. If he had not when he spoke, he did now.

'I'm sorry,' he murmured. 'Of course. If he can tell us, I intend to go there straight away.'

'Another excellent idea,' she agreed.

He merely smiled.

★   ★   ★

Peter kept his word, and even before breakfast he walked to the stationmaster's house. He returned home by the time Mariah was up, ready to travel and with her case packed.

'Well?' she asked as he came into the dining room.

'Yes,' he said with a very slight smile. He sat down and poured himself a cup of tea.

92

'Grandfather went to Brocklehurst, about forty miles away. He came back the same day, on the last train. The stationmaster said he looked tired and very grim. He barely spoke, which was unusual for him. That's why Mr Phillips remembered it so well.'

Mariah said nothing. There was both relief inside her, because they were clearly on the right track, but also pain. Cullen must have been very distressed to be brief with an old friend.

'I got us two tickets, but are you sure you still want to come? It's possible we will have to stay overnight . . . '

She gave him a look that froze the question before he finished it.

'Very well,' he agreed. 'We will take the gig, because of the cases. Will you be ready in time for the nine thirty?'

'I am ready now,' she replied. 'But by all means, finish your tea.'

He did not even attempt to hide his amusement, or the gleam of excitement in his eyes. At last they had something to do.

$\star$ $\star$ $\star$

It was a strange feeling sitting in the plush upholstered seats, Mariah next to the window. She looked out at the bleak, midwinter scenery as the train whistle blew and the last doors slammed and they began to move out of the station. In minutes they were travelling through bare fields, ploughed into deep furrows. The copses of trees were leafless and dark, their beauty harsh against a wind-racked sky, clouds piling heavy along the horizon. Rain drifted against the windows, then cleared again.

Mariah could not help her mind wandering back to imagine Cullen on this same journey twenty years ago. He would have looked out on exactly these scenes, and he too would have found them beautiful. These fields might have changed their crops, but the long shallow rise and fall of the land would be exactly the same, the curve of the track, the constantly changing views. Most of the farms were hundreds of years old, the copses of trees even older. Here and there were stretches of the ancient woodland that must have been here in Saxon times, or even Roman.

That would be what Cullen would have been thinking too. He loved the land in all its moods.

The clouds broke a little and sent shafts of bright, cold sunlight through. In the distance, higher hills were capped with snow. If it grew any colder, they would have it everywhere by Christmas Day. Children would like that. They would play in it, build snowmen, take out sleds and career down the hillsides, shouting with excitement.

She and Peter did not talk. Perhaps they had already said all there was to say on the subject of the journey, and nothing else seemed to matter now.

What had Cullen been thinking? What had sent him on this winding, rattling journey? What had he learned that had cost him his life? Was that why Peter had tried again to dissuade her from coming? If he was right, and she had argued with him, briefly, then better she be killed than he. He was Cullen's grandson, and in some ways so very like him. He was only thirty, and at the beginning of his life. She had no wish to die, not yet, but she was old, and if necessary she expected to have the courage to stop Durward hurting Peter, whatever the cost to herself.

She refused to think of it any more. The thought was frightening. She was very far from ready to face whatever lay beyond death. She still had so much to undo! The only thing more frightening still would be to fail in this.

They reached Brocklehurst and alighted on to the platform, a little bigger than the one at Haslemere, and considerably busier. Peter was carrying both her case and his own. He managed to put them both in one hand, and took her arm. She objected, and he ignored her, but with a smile.

'We don't even know where we're going!' she protested, using her umbrella as a walking stick this morning. It, too, could be an effective weapon, should they require it.

'I do,' he told her, taking even firmer hold of her arm. 'We will begin with the local vicarage. That is surely where Grandfather would have begun.'

They put the cases in the left-luggage office at the station, and walked together along the road past houses and shops towards the distant spire of the church, rising clearly above the rooftops. The wind was cold in their faces but at least, at the moment, it was not raining.

Was this a fool's errand? Cullen had discovered something twenty years ago, but would anyone remember now? Would they even be willing to spend their time talking to two strangers asking questions? There were several people in the street, shopping, talking to each other, carrying parcels ready to give as gifts. The inn was decorated with wreaths and garlands, and there was a happy noise issuing from the door as people came in and out.

They passed the postman twice. He was whistling cheerfully but he moved so swiftly he merely called ''Appy Christmas!' and went on without hesitating.

They found the church after only one misdirection, not having taken into account that the road was dog-legged and they were obliged to retrace their steps and turn the opposite way.

The vicarage was a sprawling, comfortable-looking house with dormer windows in the roof and a plume of smoke rising from the chimney. It too was decked with wreaths of holly and red ribbons at the door.

'They aren't going to like this,' Peter said, but he did not hesitate in his stride. He glanced at Mariah, drew in his breath as if to speak, then decided better of it. He lifted the brass knocker and let it fall, then stepped back.

He was about to do it a second time when the door opened and a plump woman wearing a white apron opened it. Her hands were freshly washed but there was still flour up her arms and a smear of jam on one sleeve.

'I'm sorry to disturb you,' Peter said

immediately, smiling and looking at her directly. 'I know you must be very busy, but we need help, and it cannot wait long. We have come some distance to have a word with the vicar.'

The woman looked at him with a slight frown. 'I'm not sure what I can do,' she said apologetically. She turned to Mariah, perhaps concerned that she was not well. She was tired and pale, and no doubt looked all of her years. 'You'd better come in,' the woman went on. 'It's a cruel wind, and that's for certain.' She stepped back and pulled the door wider open.

'Thank you.' Peter offered Mariah his arm and she accepted it.

The woman led them to the kitchen, a large room with a high ceiling from which was suspended an airing rail on a pulley. Over the working bench hung several strings of onions and dried herbs. A Welsh dresser was stacked with dishes, and there were copper pans gleaming along the walls. The whole room was warm and scented with spices, as if someone were cooking rich and comforting food. They passed a woman with a bucket and scrubbing brush, who nodded an acknowledgement to their hostess. Was the welcoming woman the vicar's wife, and the flour on her arms indicated that she was doing her own cooking?

'You look perished.' The woman in the apron regarded Mariah with concern. She was possibly in her fifties herself, but she was at least twenty-five years younger than Mariah. 'Sit down and have a cup of tea,' she offered. 'I was just about to make one. The vicar is out, but he won't be very long. Everyone wants to speak to him about something this time of year. Christmas is a good time for families, and a bad one too. Old memories are not always easy.'

She offered a hard-backed kitchen chair to Mariah, and a stool to Peter, then without waiting to ask, she pulled the kettle off the side of the huge stove and set it on the hob to boil. Then she opened up the fire door and gave the embers a good poke.

'Have you been in the village long, ma'am?' Peter asked.

'About fifteen years,' she replied. Then she turned and looked at him more closely, studying his face. 'It's something serious, isn't it?' she asked.

'Yes, Mrs . . . ?' He wanted the courtesy of calling her by name, but he had no idea what it was.

'Mrs Fraser,' she told him.

'Peter Wesley. And this is my aunt Mariah, Mrs Ellison.'

'How do you do?' Mrs Fraser said warmly. 'Is it the matter of a spiritual problem that's brought you here?'

'Not entirely,' Peter answered before Mariah could say anything. 'An old wrong that has resurfaced and is going to cause new grief, a great deal of it. My grandfather died exactly twenty years ago. He visited Brocklehurst the day before his death. We now think that he learned something while he was here that affected him very deeply — and affected someone else with such a fear that . . . that it will not be buried.

Perhaps there is great evil, and perhaps not. For many people's sakes, we must discover as much truth as possible.'

'Twenty years ago.' She shook her head. 'We were not here then. And I'm afraid the vicar before my husband passed away several years ago now. People come and go, you know. More than ever these days. Young people go to the cities. New ones come here.'

'My grandfather spoke to someone here, and whatever was said changed his mind about defending a case,' Peter told her.

'And he wouldn't tell you?' Mrs Fraser shook her head, pursing her lips a little. 'You know, Mr Wesley, there are things one learns, in the course of one's calling, that you are not permitted to repeat. Sometimes that can be very hard. You say, 'defend a case'? Was your grandfather a lawyer?'

'Yes. And I dare say he could not have told anyone, but if it were common knowledge, not in any way a secret, then he could have . . . '

She shook her head again. 'Then if he would not tell anyone, it must have been a confidence of some sort. I'm sorry.'

'He couldn't tell anyone because he was murdered!' Mariah said quickly, her own voice almost choking her. Taking the same train journey as Cullen, through the same winter fields and woods, almost the same day of the year, it was as if they had travelled in time, and any moment he could come in through the door and join them. It was a trick of time and circumstance that they were here without him.

Mrs Fraser turned pale and sat down very suddenly on the stool behind her.

'Oh, my dear! How very dreadful. No wonder you are so distressed.'

As if deliberately to interrupt her, the kettle on the hob began to whistle shrilly with increasing volume.

Peter stood up and took it off the heat.

Mrs Fraser, too, rose to her feet. 'Thank you. Oh, I'm so sorry. How terrible . . . ' She moved to make a pot of tea, finding things in cupboards, picking clean cups off the Welsh dresser stacked with china.

'We need to know, because someone is trying to open the case again, and cast blame on my grandmother,' Peter went on.

Mrs Fraser almost dropped a cup. 'On your grandmother?'

'Yes. It is for her sake that we need to know the truth. Who could we speak to that was here twenty years ago?'

'More than that,' Mariah interrupted, 'Mr Wesley's grandfather learned something, almost certainly about Dr Durward — '

This time Mrs Fraser did drop the cup, but caught it again before it rolled off the dresser on to the floor.

'Oh dear!' She took a deep breath. 'Oh dear,' she said again. Then before Peter or Mariah could say anything, she went on, 'You should speak to Bessie Collins. Constable Collins is the local policeman now, for the last eleven or twelve years anyway. Bessie's his wife, and her father was constable before John Collins came here.

Ask Bessie. She can tell you some of the things that happened years ago, even before the time your grandfather came to ask.'

'Thank you,' Mariah said immediately. She was just getting nicely warmed and she would love a cup of tea, but this was real hope, at last. But she was perfectly ready to abandon it and leave immediately. 'Thank you. Where do we find her? Will she see us, do you think?'

'I'll send her a note,' Mrs Fraser said. 'I know she's busy, but I'm thinking this is an old injustice that needs mending. What's Christmas about, if it isn't about hope, and giving a hand where it's needed? Setting things right, before the end of the old year. Just let me get this tea right, and a piece of shortbread or two, and then I'll send Alice round to the constable's house.'

* ★ *

Actually it would be time for high tea, about five o'clock, before Bessie Collins would be able to spare time to speak to Mariah and Peter without repeated interruption. Mariah waited impatiently as she and Peter took luncheon at the inn. They booked in for the night, as it would almost certainly be necessary, and he walked back to the station and fetched their cases. Then they spent the afternoon in the very pleasant lounge turning over and over all the possibilities of what Bessie Collins might be able to tell them. What would they do if it amounted to nothing?

'It won't!' Mariah said, more to strengthen herself than Peter. 'Cullen learned something

101

. . . something so bad that he couldn't ignore it. He had to tell Durward that he could not defend him. Surely that can only mean that he knew Durward was guilty?'

'I hope so,' Peter said ruefully. 'But there are other possibilities.'

'Such as what?' Mariah demanded.

'Such as a secret about someone else, I suppose.'

'How would that stop him defending Durward? Are you saying that that vile man is innocent? Then why kill Cullen? That makes no sense.'

'Perhaps it implicated someone else?' he said miserably.

'Like your grandmother? Nonsense! She may have been . . . unwise . . . but that is hardly on an equal footing with kidnapping, raping and murdering Christina Abbott. No!' She closed her eyes. 'I know something of people who have . . . appetites they dare not own, and cannot control. And I am sure in my own mind that whoever killed Christina is such a man.' She opened her eyes and stared at him, defying him to argue with her. 'In fact if he was innocent, Cullen would have done everything necessary to prove it. He might have hated it, but he would not have shrunk from it. You know that as well as I do!'

'I'm not sure I know anything as well as you do, Aunt Mariah, but I believe it. I am just afraid that there is something else involved that we don't know about.'

She did not ask him what he suspected. All

sorts of vague ideas loomed in her mind, dark shadows at the edges of thought, but she dreaded looking at them. She would wait until at least some of them had softened, or taken a shape she could deal with. It was the unknown that paralysed the will to fight.

Time dragged by, and then suddenly, when she was not ready for it, Peter looked up from the newspaper he had been reading, smiled, and rose to his feet.

'Let's go and have high tea with the constable's wife.' He offered Mariah his arm.

She stood up, a little stiffly, but determined to do it without assistance. She took his arm lightly, although she would like to have clung on to him.

Outside in the street it was dark already and the lamps were lit. The hard wind had driven away the clouds and there was a slick of frost on the pavement. She was glad now to have hold of his arm, in case she slipped. She noticed that he walked quite slowly, so she did not have to hurry more than was comfortable.

In the past she had envied Rowena her happy marriage. She had learned over time not to let it eat away at her. Better to dream than have the reality, and see it fade from joy into mere acceptability. The worst of all would be to have it, and then lose it by ill-temper, carelessness, or simply failing to treasure what mattered. She had observed that time and again also. There was little in life more bitter than disillusion. Only treasure lost through one's own selfishness was worse.

But she wished she had a grandson like Peter.

Or perhaps a friend was just as good. There was no duty in such a friendship, only gentleness that was real, without obligation, just gratitude for its value.

They were cold by the time they arrived at the constable's house, next to the police station and easy to find, once they were on the right street. The lights were all on, including the streetlamp just outside. Garlands of holly and ivy, decked with ribbons, hung on the door and on the gate.

They walked carefully up the paved path; the stones were distinctly icy now. Just as they reached the door, it opened ahead of them. Clearly, someone had been awaiting their arrival.

A small girl of perhaps six smiled up. She was missing a couple of teeth, giving her a unique charm. Her hair was tied up with a large red ribbon, like those twined in the wreaths.

'You're here for tea,' she said, pleased with her knowledge. 'Mama says please come in.' She held the door open.

'Thank you,' Mariah accepted, feeling the warmth close around her, not only of the fires in the house, but of safety, and the child's excitement at Christmas, still magic for her. 'I like your ribbon,' she added. 'It matches the wreaths.'

The child smiled widely, her eyes shining. 'Yes, it does!' She took a breath. 'Thank you,' she added, then bit her lip. She had very nearly forgotten her manners. She looked shyly at Peter.

He was not used to children, and he spoke to her as if she were an adult.

'How do you do? My name is Peter. What is yours?' He offered his hand. She took it carefully. 'Hello, Peter.'

'Hello . . . ?' he waited.

She looked down, then up again. 'Francesca, but they call me Fanny.'

'May I call you Fanny?' he asked. 'Although I think Francesca is a lovely name.'

'You can call me Francesca, if you like?' she offered.

'I accept. How do you do, Francesca?'

She giggled, then took his hand, just for a moment.

Mariah saw a woman standing in the doorway ahead of them. She was handsome, with the same dark chestnut hair as the child.

'Mrs Collins?' Mariah asked. 'This is very gracious of you. I hope we are not inconveniencing you a great deal. If this were not urgent we would not disturb you without warning, and so close to Christmas.'

'I understand,' Mrs Collins said gravely. 'Excuse Fanny. She wanted to be the one to welcome you, and show off her dress.'

'Quite understandable,' Mariah nodded. 'And the ribbons. If I had been so pretty, I would wear ribbons too.'

Francesca blushed with pleasure, and stood a little closer to her mother's skirts.

They were introduced to her younger brother, who was far more interested in his train set than any visitors. Peter duly admired it, quite genuinely. Then the children went to their tea in the large, warm kitchen, and Peter and Mariah were shown into the parlour where the table was laid for four.

'I don't know whether my husband will be home for tea or not,' Mrs Collins said with apology. 'I'm afraid he's often late. There's always something, in a village like this. Mostly it's not crime so much as something lost, even a stray animal. We'll start without him, if you don't mind. I know you may have a train to catch, and the last one is not so very late. Although if you need to stay overnight, the inn is quite good, and your tickets will be good for several days.'

'Thank you,' Peter accepted for both of them. 'We have already booked rooms at the inn, just in case.'

She frowned. 'That's good. Mrs Fraser said your enquiry is very serious.' Her face lost its warmth and the pleasure of hospitality. She had been a policeman's daughter, and now a policeman's wife. She knew there could be tragedy, even in the quietest and outwardly gentlest of places.

Mariah sat where she was invited, as did Peter, and Bessie Collins offered them anything they asked for from the plentiful table. There was a large baked ham, sliced bacon and egg pie with a thick pastry crust to it, an apple tart and a jug of cream. There were also two kinds of cake, both clearly home baked. One was a sponge, the other a rich fruit cake, sagging a little in the middle. It was what Mariah's mother, more than half a century ago, would have called 'sad', meaning it was heavier in the middle, and a little richer and moister than was considered perfect. Actually, if you only knew it, that was the best part.

As soon as they were served, Peter acquainted Bessie briefly with their reason for coming. He did not speak of Durward with condemnation, as if they knew he were guilty, only the barest facts of his trial and Cullen Wesley's acceptance of his defence, then at the last moment, his refusal to continue with it.

'And you say he came here to Brocklehurst the day before?' Bessie said.

'Yes,' Peter agreed. 'We know that from the stationmaster, and from the vicar's wife here. We learned it only yesterday. But time is short.'

'And now Durward intends to raise the whole matter again.' Her face was bleak. 'I'm surprised. He must feel very . . . confident.'

'He wishes to marry,' Mariah pointed out. She did not bother to keep the acid out of her voice. 'Into money, I believe. He must lay this business to rest before he does so.' She took a mouthful of ham and the delicately flavoured potatoes. She ate it and swallowed before continuing. 'I am not sure whether it is a matter of striking first, or if he has some reason to believe the matter will arise again, if he does nothing. We need to stop him . . . '

'Indeed,' Bessie said fervently. 'We couldn't! And, heaven knows, my father tried. I don't remember it. I was only a child, about Francesca's age, when your father came, and I was only just born when it happened here.'

Peter froze.

Mariah felt the food in her mouth all but impossible to swallow. She did so only with difficulty. 'It . . . ?' She hardly dared ask, and yet it was what she had expected. It was the dark certainty that hovered on the edge of her mind. Her own experience taught her that such terrible hungers do not come out of the night suddenly. They had begun as imaginings, dreams, then little realities, like the first drops of rain in a squall that will eventually drown everything.

'We lost a girl, too,' Bessie said quietly, all the light gone from her face. There was distress in her eyes. 'She was thirteen. They didn't find her body until a week later. Only God can know what that child endured first. I have days when I look at Fanny, and I can hardly bear it for Mrs Catherwood, or any woman who has lost her child.' She laid down her knife and fork, as if the idea of eating were suddenly repellent. 'The Catherwoods moved away. I think they might have gone abroad, eventually. I can't blame them. To look at these woods and fields must be more than they can bear.'

'I'm sorry to ask you to remember this,' Peter said gently. 'But we have to stop him, if we can.'

'We tried!' Bessie said with a sudden, fierce insistence. 'We did everything we knew how.' She pushed her rich hair back from her brow, pulling at it hard. 'I say 'we' as if I were part of it, but the whole village felt that, even though it was twenty-five years ago now. I saw it in my father's face as I was growing up. He watched us so tightly I used to lose my temper with him. Of course I didn't understand. No one told me the real story behind it until just a few years ago. I was a grown woman with a girl of my own before he would tell me.' She stopped.

Neither Peter nor Mariah prompted her.

For several moments they ate in silence. It seemed to Mariah almost blasphemous to eat when they were speaking of such things, but not eating would help no one. They needed their strength to think clearly, to keep going beyond weariness or defeat. Losing the will or the clarity of thought to fight would be another victory for Durward.

In the silence her mind slipped back to the other tragedies she had known, particularly the loss of one of her granddaughters to a compulsive, insane mind twisted with guilt and seemingly unable to stop the terrible violence within it.

'We must stop him!' she said abruptly. 'Our own comfort is neither here nor there.'

Bessie Collins and Peter both looked startled.

'I'm sorry,' Mariah said grimly. 'But one of my granddaughters died at the hand of someone whose mind was obsessed by . . . desires that were . . . not acceptable. They don't go away.'

Peter put his hand on hers, gently. It was warm, and she felt ice inside her, freezing more dangerously every moment. Did he imagine she was going to speak of her husband? She wasn't. That was still untouchable in her mind. Peter probably knew nothing of this other violence in her life, other loss.

'The man who killed Christina Abbott in Haslemere,' she said with an effort, 'from what you say, killed a child here also. They were twenty and twenty-five years ago. Do you imagine that was the end of it?' She met Bessie's blue eyes and saw the grief in them, and the sudden pity. 'I wish I didn't have to say that,' she added.

'I know,' Bessie murmured. 'I know. Of course you are right. I have no idea if anyone will speak now. They wouldn't then. There's only Mina Johnson left who was here then. She could have spoken, I believe. But she denied it. She and her husband owned one of the bigger farms over at the south side of the village. He's gone, and their sons have it now. She lives in a cottage about half a mile from here.'

'What could she say? If she chose to?' Peter asked.

Bessie looked down at her plate. 'She said it could not have been Owen Durward who killed the girl. She was ill, and he came to treat her at that time. It all fitted in . . . and no one else was ever found to blame. It . . . it poisoned everything, because we all looked sideways at each other for ages after that, so my father told me. He broke his heart trying to find the answer, but he never did.'

'Could we speak to him?' Mariah asked urgently. 'Just in case in the details there is something. It only takes one thread you can pull hard enough to unravel the whole cloth.'

Bessie bit her lip. 'You don't give up, do you! I'll take you to see him, but only if you let me stay with you. I won't have him upset more than he can take. It twisted him, that. It was the one thing he failed at, that he still can't forget.'

'Maybe we can finish it now?' Mariah said.

She created a hope in her voice that she did not feel, but it was an effort, a piece of play-acting such as she had never forced herself into before.

Bessie still hesitated.

'He'll do it again,' Mariah said. 'He may have already, and got away with it.' She thought of adding something about Francesca, and decided that was too far. At least it was now.

'Apple pie?' Bessie offered. 'I think I'll cut a piece for John, then we can take a nice big piece for my father. It's one of his favourites.'

'What an excellent idea,' Mariah agreed. 'Will he have cream, or should we take a little of that, too?'

Bessie smiled. 'You're a canny one,' she said briefly.

★　★　★

It was nearly an hour later when the constable came home. Bessie served his dinner and left Peter to talk to him, and she and Mariah put on their heavy coats and took a shopping bag with a jar of thick cream and a very generous slice of the apple pie, still warm from the oven. They set out into the now bitterly cold evening, arm in arm so as not to risk sliding on the ice-rimed pavements.

The new moon was high in a clear sky and the stars were so low that for a moment Mariah had the illusion that they were actually tangled in the bare branches of the tallest trees. It was easy to believe in Christmas, all the stories and the legends that added to its wealth. Did they sometimes lose the greatest gifts among the smaller ones?

They did not speak as they walked. It took concentration to keep one's footing, and the cold air was sharp when drawn into the lungs if one breathed in quickly.

The retired constable lived on the far side of the village, in a cottage that stood by itself in a neat garden. It was without leaves or flowers now, everything gone back into the earth to sleep until spring. Mariah imagined the new growth bursting forth: snowdrops by the end of January, then small irises, dark purple. In March there would be daffodils, then paler yellow primroses on the sloping banks of the fields facing the sun. There would be pussy willows by the streams, and hazel catkins in the hedges, then chestnut candles later, and bluebell woods. There was nothing closer to heaven than wild pear blossom in the trees, before the leaves came, and the earth so carpeted with bluebells there was nowhere to put one's feet.

She missed all that in the city, but it was all there in memory. And on the other hand she had company and a good garden in the summer. The roses were marvellous, rich and lush, perfuming the still air.

They walked up the path and knocked on the door. It was opened by an elderly man, grown a little heavy with age, but still upright. His face lit with pleasure when he saw Bessie, and the pie and cream. He offered the visitors tea, which was politely declined.

'Papa, Mrs Ellison has come about an old

case, and I think you will want to hear what she has to say. It's about Owen Durward.' Bessie bit her lip. 'I'm sorry.'

The old man's face became suddenly bleak, and he regarded Mariah with a cold, very judging eye.

'Sit down, Mrs Ellison,' he said, now very much the retired policeman. 'Tell me, what has brought you here?'

Mariah accepted the offered seat, and told him very briefly, almost as if she were making a statement to the police in the most formal sense. She told him of Cullen Wesley's acceptance of the case to defend Durward, then his visit here to Brocklehurst, and his violent death the following day, after he had said he could not continue to represent Durward.

'I heard of it,' the old man said gravely. 'Forgive me speaking of it, but I also heard the rumour that his wife was suspected because of some dalliance she had had, and they had quarrelled over it. Someone else defended Durward, and he was found not guilty.' The grief in his eyes and the tightness in his face said more clearly than words what he thought of that.

Mariah did not answer immediately. She studied his expression, the good nature in him clouded over by his one crippling failure. She also saw that even though he was trying to disguise it, he still had a flicker of hope that it could be retrieved, even a little. Bessie would not have brought someone to him if there were nothing at all she could do.

He waited.

'Do you believe he killed the girl here in Brocklehurst?' Mariah asked finally. 'I know you could not prove it.'

He did not equivocate. 'Yes, I do.'

'And did you tell Cullen Wesley that when he came here the day before his death?' she went on.

'Yes. I told him all I knew. I'm . . . I'm sorry now that I did. Perhaps he would still be alive if I had said nothing.'

That thought had flickered through Mariah's mind also, like lightning leaving charred trees behind it. But it was too late now. And how would it have changed Cullen if he had obtained Durward's acquittal, and then learned that he was guilty?

She said that now to the old man. 'And he would not have thanked you for that,' she added. 'You gave him the truth you knew, and he acted on it as he believed to be right.'

He looked at her closely, studying her face as she had studied his. 'Why did he retire from the case?' he asked. 'Because he believed me, and he thought Durward had done it a second time. The cases were similar in all the wretched details that mattered. He couldn't defend a man, knowing he had done it before, and would almost certainly do it again. We both failed in that. If I had not told him, he would never have known, and he could have defended Durward with a clear conscience, serving just as he was bound to do.'

'Perhaps he knew something more.' She took his point. 'He no longer had the innocence of not knowing. I wonder what he said to Durward, and what Durward said to him that perhaps changed his mind.' She imagined the scene. Durward had got away with it once, and believed he could again. Had he told Cullen as much?

'Maybe he'd thought of a way of seeming to defend Durward, and yet making certain he lost. He would remain within the law.' The old man was clearly turning over the ideas in his mind.

'You could have charged him, if Mrs Johnson hadn't said he was with her,' Bessie pointed out. 'She was lying, wasn't she?'

'Oh, yes,' the old man agreed. 'But she never backed down.'

'What was she like, Mrs Johnson, twenty-five years ago?' Mariah asked with a sudden flare of interest. 'Pretty? Well mannered, happily married, but occasionally maybe a little bored? Was her husband a man who loved her, but sometimes took for granted her contentment, her interests, her need for admiration now and then?' Had she gone too far? Was that deliberately unkind? At least Peter was not here to understand to whom she was referring.

'You knew her?' the old constable asked with the very slightest smile.

'No, but I know women like her.'

The old man was staring at her now. 'Are you saying that that is what happened in Haslemere, Mrs Ellison? Someone was . . . coerced into silence?'

'Not exactly,' she replied. If she had not felt the warmth in him, and the gravity, this would have been appallingly different. 'I'm afraid it was

115

both better and worse than that. I don't think
. . . the person in question would have remained
silent. Cullen Wesley was killed, and it was made
to look as if his wife could have been responsible.
Durward actually spread it around that that was
what happened.' She took a breath. 'Little by
little, of course. A word here, a silence there,
where an explanation would have closed the
matter. She was never charged, but the silent
accusation never completely went away.'

'I see. And how can I help, Mrs Ellison?'

'Give me more of the circumstances of the
first woman who was bullied into lying for him.'

He shook his head. 'She won't tell the truth
now. She has everything to lose and nothing to
gain by admitting she lied twenty-five years ago.'

'Possibly. But please allow me to try.' Should
she tell him she would go and look for the
woman herself, if he did not help her? It would
sound like a threat. 'Please?'

'Do you wish me to come with you?' he asked.

She considered it for barely a moment. 'No,
thank you. She knows you, and may well care
what you think of her. In her place, I would. She
does not know me, so what I think will matter
nothing to her, once I am gone.'

'There's wisdom in that,' he agreed. 'Very well.
I'll give you directions to her house. I suggest
you go in the morning. She keeps chickens and a
pony, and she will be up early to feed them. She
will care for the animals before she leaves,
regardless of whatever else she intends to do for
the day.'

'Thank you.' She stood up. She had done too

much walking and she was stiff. 'I am sure Bessie will tell you if I have any success. I am much obliged to you.'

She and Bessie walked back to pick up Peter, say good night to Fanny and her brother, and walk a little more slowly back through the darkness towards the inn. She was grateful that they had already booked rooms for the night and she was surprised how glad she was to have a light supper and go to bed.

★   ★   ★

In the morning, Mariah woke wondering where on earth she was. The whole room seemed unfamiliar, the heavy curtains, the open suitcase on the ottoman, the wine-coloured carpet. It took several moments for her to recall the previous evening. She had been full of determination when she had spoken to the retired constable, whose name she recalled as Harris. Now it all seemed like a hopeless task. No one had caught Durward the first time or the second. Two girls were horribly dead, and Cullen, dear Cullen, whom she had cared for so much, had been killed as well — and Owen Durward had walked away free.

Now he was back. How did old, plain, charmless Mariah Ellison imagine she was going to stop him?

Even as she finished the thought, instead of self-pity or even anger, there came an answer that was clear in her mind: exactly because she was old and plain and had no charm at all, he would take her lightly. He was too arrogant to be afraid of her! That was the one card she had, and if she played it cleverly enough, it could be sufficient to win.

She got up, washed and dressed, necessarily in the outer clothes she had worn the day before, but they were perfectly acceptable. She went down to the dining room for breakfast and found Peter waiting for her. He stood to welcome her, and pull out her chair for her to be seated.

'Are you all right?' he asked with some concern.

'Do I look unwell?' she replied a little more sharply than she had intended. In fact, she had something of a headache.

'No, you look fine,' he replied with his sudden, charming smile. 'But so do I, and I feel very rough around the edges.'

'Oh. I'm sorry.' She meant it. She had temporarily forgotten that Cullen had been the grandfather he had loved all his early childhood, when his own parents had been so soon lost. She had not given enough thought to his feelings, or the fact that he surely needed this clearing of his name even more than she did, or perhaps Rowena either.

'I plan to go and see this woman Mrs Johnson this morning,' she told him, with as much good cheer as she could manufacture. 'I think I might get further with her if I see her alone. Whatever she has to say, it could embarrass her to say it in front of a young man. You would not mean to intimidate her, but you might still do so. If I am right, then it was your family who was injured by her silence . . . and of course the Abbotts.' She wished she could add something more to what she said. She was not a woman who called upon God, or ever referred to him, but just now the thought came naturally to her, it just did not come to speech.

'How are you going to get there?' he asked. 'Would you not prefer that I accompany you? Or if necessary we could hire some conveyance?' His concern was unmistakable in his eyes.

'Thank you, that would be very pleasant,' she accepted. 'But I believe it is not very far. Then I shall walk back when I am satisfied I can learn no more from her.'

'Then I will walk with you.' It was a statement, not an offer.

'Thank you,' she said graciously.

It was actually a good mile's walk, but this day was sunny and the centre of the path where others had already trodden in the grit made it safe, if one took care.

They spoke of other things on the journey. She asked him about his life, his work, his pleasures, and she found herself liking him more and more with each answer. There was an enthusiasm in him she liked very much. But she still could not allow him to come into the house. It was certainly true that his presence might well deter Mrs Johnson from speaking of things that were sad and embarrassing, but quite apart from that, Mariah intended to press this woman very hard to tell the truth, and she would use any means required to achieve that. Some of them she would rather Peter did not see. There was no time left for restraint. Apart from protecting Rowena now, and gaining justice for the past, for two dead girls, and for Cullen, there was the matter of seeing Durward arrested and thus prevented from continuing to do such things. That was the most important of all.

And another thought came, like the touch of ice — who else might there have been that they did not know of? Has he really been restrained, hurt no one, over the twenty years since Christina? Stopping him now was immeasurably more important than settling the past. Her husband had never changed, never lessened his cruelty or the need to hurt, to frighten. To dominate. She refused to allow that thought any more. It no longer sickened her, and she was able, for the first time in her life, to push away the humiliation. Even in her dreams, it was no longer there. Now she was a fighter, standing up for the oppressed and ill-used and those two girls who had lost everything.

When they arrived at the Johnson home, Mariah thanked Peter and watched him walk away, and then she knocked on the front door. She barely glanced around the garden. It was winter, bare earth, a couple of laurel bushes, mounds beneath, which would be dormant roots of perennials that would come forth in the spring. The door opened and a handsome woman of about fifty stood looking at her with surprise.

'Good morning, Mrs Johnson,' Mariah said courteously. She must not allow her tension to show; it would alarm the woman, as it should.

'You have been recommended to me by both the vicar's wife, and the constable's wife, for some advice.'

'Oh, really?' Mrs Johnson looked startled, but not at all displeased. She stepped back to allow Mariah to come in, then she led the way through to the kitchen where she had clearly been busy. She offered Mariah a seat, which she accepted. A very large pail stood on the bench near the sink, and potato peelings, cabbage stalks and broken egg shells lay around it. There were also some old carrot skins, and what could have been turnip peelings with them.

Mrs Johnson saw Mariah's glance. 'I was about to feed the chickens,' she explained. 'And collect the eggs.'

'I'm sorry to disturb you,' Mariah said. Then an idea came to her. She dared not think of it too clearly or she could find too many reasons not to suggest it. But sharing incurred friendship, obligation, kindness more than was merely good manners. 'Perhaps I could help?' she offered.

Mrs Johnson was taken aback. There was a certain pride in her face, a pleasure, not a haughtiness. 'Thank you.' She looked Mariah up and down from her handsome dark winter coat with its fur trimmings, to her polished black boots. She was an old woman, but she had always had trim ankles and one of her indulgences was well-cut boots. Elegant would not be an exaggeration.

'I'd hate you to get those handsome boots soiled,' Mrs Johnson said, shaking her head.

'Nonsense! They clean very well.' Trying to

hide the effort, and a little stiffness from too much walking of late, Mariah rose from the kitchen chair. 'I would be delighted to help you. Perhaps it will save an extra journey for you.' She averted her eyes from the pail and the mess on the chopping board.

'Thank you,' Mrs Johnson accepted. 'I must admit it gets heavy at times, and it's always pleasant to have company. Where do you come from, Mrs Ellison? Have you just moved into Brocklehurst?'

Mariah was prepared to bide her time. She would have only this one chance. If she spoiled it, there would not be another.

'No, I am just visiting. I have dear friends in Haslemere.' She looked at the mess in the pail, to which Mrs Johnson was now adding the pieces of vegetable on the bench. 'Do chickens really eat all these?' she asked.

'Oh, bless you, yes. I'll add some grain, of course, but all this is good for them. A bit of everything is what makes the eggs so good.'

Mariah listened as Mrs Johnson described the merits of different kinds of chickens. She knew many of her own birds by individual name as well as breed. She mixed the mash vigorously, added some very hot water, then put it all into two pails, and went to the door once more. Mariah picked up the other pail and followed her, trying very hard not to let her skirt be marked by the exterior of the pail and its stains of usage.

The air outside was sharp, but still bright, and she was careful where she put her feet on the stepping stones down the garden path to the henhouse, and the wire-enclosed space around it. Apparently chickens had an urgent desire to escape.

'Now . . . in there.' Mrs Johnson indicated a wooden trough. First she tipped the contents of her own pail into it and there was a wild scuffle of chickens, feathers, hysterical squawking, and then finally some sort of order as the birds fought each other for the food.

'There.' Mrs Johnson indicated another empty trough and Mariah tipped up her pail to fill it. She had not counted on the excitement of the birds. One flew from a high perch, somewhere above her line of sight, and banged into her. She dropped the pail and it turned upside down on her feet. Seconds later she was attacked on all sides by birds diving and charging each other to get the scraps. Mariah had a moment's panic, then told herself, with disgust, not to be frightened by a flock of chickens. She managed not to cry out.

'Oh dear,' Mrs Johnson said patiently. 'I'm afraid they're a bit . . . a bit greedy. Stop it!' she commanded with considerable authority. 'Goldie! Stop it! Big Red!' she called a few more by name, which as far as Mariah could see, had no effect at all. But generally they moved to the troughs and there was a return of relative peace.

'That's better,' Mrs Johnson said approvingly. Then she looked at Mariah. 'Would you like to help me collect the eggs? While they're all busy eating is the best time.'

Mariah looked at the long, sharp beaks of the

hens, and the longer and even sharper claws on their feet. 'Of course,' she answered in a voice a little higher than usual.

It was a highly hazardous affair, but they found over a dozen warm, brown eggs, all of handsome size, and escaped with no more than straw in their skirts, and a few marks of hot, wet meal and a couple of scratches.

Back in the kitchen, Mrs Johnson put the kettle on and, while it was coming to the boil, carefully placed half a dozen of the new eggs into a small basket for Mariah. She put the rest into a bin with a wooden lid.

'Oh,' she exclaimed when she saw Mariah's surprise. 'My white cat loves to fish for them with his paw and fling them around. All the ones that break, he eats. Cats are great egg thieves, you know. Now what is it Bessie thinks I can help you with?' She turned away to take the kettle off the hob and make the tea.

It gave Mariah a moment to clear her thoughts. The chickens had put the whole issue out of her mind. The woman had been kind. Mariah had already formed a liking for her. Such informal ease was unlike the acquaintances she had in the city, and she was loath to break it cruelly.

'I have been staying in Haslemere with an old friend,' she began, knowing she could not dither around indefinitely. The matter was urgent, and terrible. It would be so much easier to give up now. She could really say that she had tried. She must commit herself, so she could not turn back. 'Mrs Rowena Wesley,' she went on. 'She is going through a very difficult time. Twenty years ago this Christmas, her husband, Cullen Wesley, was murdered. I dare say you heard of it at the time?'

Mrs Johnson froze, her back stiff, the kettle in her hand half poured into the teapot. 'Yes,' she said after what seemed like seconds had gone by. 'It was very dreadful.'

'It is all being raised again,' Mariah continued. 'And the unkindest of people are suggesting that she was to blame.'

Mrs Johnson put the kettle down slowly, paying attention to what she was doing, in case she scalded herself. Finally, she turned to face Mariah. The colour had drained from her cheeks. 'Why would they say that? Wasn't he . . . defending Owen Durward? Surely they can't blame her for that? It was his job!'

'Of course it was,' Mariah agreed quickly. 'But he visited Brocklehurst, spending the whole day here, and he learned something that made him change his mind. The next day he told Durward that he could not continue. Then he was murdered.' She watched Mrs Johnson's face closely, every shadow of pain, memory, and fear that crossed it.

'That is terrible,' Mrs Johnson said hoarsely. 'But why would she do that?'

'She wouldn't,' Mariah agreed. 'It was Durward who suggested a reason.'

Mrs Johnson was pasty white now. She swallowed. 'What could that be? I don't understand.'

Mariah smiled, as gently as she could. She felt a pity towards this woman that was almost overwhelming. She even considered stopping, but only for an instant. Rowena needed help, and more importantly to Mariah, Peter believed in her.

'I think you might,' she said. 'She told me, with much shame now, that once she . . . flirted with him, perhaps unwisely.' She saw the scarlet rise in Mrs Johnson's cheeks and ignored it as if it were unnoticeable. 'Durward exaggerated it enormously, and said that she had lied about it, and told her husband a complete untruth about the incident. Indeed, he said that she had offered herself to him, and he had been repulsed by the idea. He said that it was in revenge for that, and his own feeling of inadequacy, that had made Cullen Wesley decline to represent Durward at his trial.'

It was several moments before Mrs Johnson responded.

'That is terrible,' she said huskily, barely able to speak.

'Yes, it is,' Mariah agreed. 'But he is a terrible man.'

'But this was not . . . '

'Not why Cullen would not defend him? Of course not,' Mariah agreed. 'He knew it was not true. He came here to Brocklehurst. He found out about the rape and murder of the girl here, in exactly the same fashion as the crime committed at Haslemere. And that although Durward had done it, he had escaped by blackmailing a decent but vulnerable woman into swearing that he was elsewhere, with her, at the time. Since he was a doctor — still is, as far

126

as I know — it was quite believable. No one thought ill of her for it.'

Mrs Johnson sank into the chair closest to her, leaving the full teapot on the side of the stove. She looked close to collapse and seemed still unable to speak.

Mariah's mind was racing, filled with rage and grief for what Durward had done to so many people, and fear that she now had to continue to shame this woman, or let him go free.

'I dare say she thought only of whom she was protecting,' she went on. 'And perhaps she even believed he was falsely accused. One time, it would be believable. But twice?' She hesitated, reluctant, but knowing she must finish. 'The murder of Christina Abbott, five years later, was exactly the same.' She lowered her voice a little. 'Except that Cullen Wesley linked the two crimes and so he had to be killed, and his wife blamed for that in the view of the village, even if not in law. That too has gone down as an unsolved crime.'

Mrs Johnson raised her head. 'But no more girls . . . children . . . ?'

'I don't know,' Mariah admitted. 'He had not been in the area. But he has come back to clear his name, because he wishes to marry there, to a woman of considerable means.'

Mrs Johnson shook her head slowly, in a denial for which she could find no words.

Mariah could not let it go. 'Appetites like that don't go away,' she said, even more softly. 'My husband had such . . . hungers. Fortunately, it was not for young girls, and did not lead to

127

murder. His violence towards me was sufficient for him.'

Mrs Johnson looked up. Her eyes were filled with misery. 'What is it you want of me? I can't undo what has been done.'

'None of us can do that,' Mariah agreed, gently now. 'If we could, perhaps we all would. I would! But we can balance the scales a little. We can save Rowena Wesley from blame, and more urgently, we can stop Durward from continuing to prosper, and perhaps kill more girls. That would be at our door, because we have the power to stop him now.'

Mrs Johnson lifted her hands helplessly, as though she were warding off a blow that might render her dizzy and disoriented. She looked stunned.

'At least we can try!' Mariah insisted. 'I may well fail alone. We may even fail together, but we will have done all we can. Are you willing to come with me?'

'I suppose I must,' Mrs Johnson said quietly. 'You won't let me stay away, will you?'

'No,' Mariah agreed. 'But you will not be alone. You may be, in the long time afterwards, when you could have acted, and it is too late.' It was harsh, and she meant it to be. She had too many years of regret not to understand the useless, relentless pain of it. 'Not everyone gets a second chance. Don't let that go by too.'

Mrs Johnson nodded.

Mariah smiled at her, then stood up and went over to the stove to bring the teapot, cups and the small jug of milk back to the table.

Peter and Mariah returned to Haslemere that afternoon, catching the second train. She had told him over lunch in a private parlour at the inn all about her visit with Mrs Johnson, and there was no more to be said now.

She sat opposite him in an otherwise empty carriage. The rhythm of the wheels over the rail ties was soothing. Mariah would like to have relaxed into it, even gone to sleep. She had not rested well through the night: old memories had come back, filled with fear and physical pain, but above all shame. But if she let sleep overcome her now, she would dream. Better to watch the countryside, even through the rain that streaked the windows.

'We must plan very carefully,' she said to Peter. 'We will only get one chance.'

'I know,' he said, looking very directly at her. 'And that also means that we have to have an alternative plan, should Mrs Johnson fail to step forward.'

That was the fear at the back of Mariah's mind. In the past, she herself had resolved to reach out and do something about her husband, threaten him that she would make his obsessive tastes public. In the end, she had lost her courage, remained silent, and been punished for her insolence for having dared to threaten him. She could understand so easily Mrs Johnson's reluctance, but it would be her stepping forward that would finally end the injustice. There were three unsolved deaths. What else had happened in the twenty years since Cullen's death they did not know. What might happen in the future lay very heavily on Mariah's mind, because preventing more deaths lay within her grasp. Surrender was not acceptable, whatever the cost.

'I don't think she will fail,' Mariah said. Then she went on rashly, 'But if she does, I will speak for her, and I will make them believe me. But, of course, that will not heal her wound of guilt, which is what I told her. Peter, we must proceed as if we know we will win. Durward can scent fear and doubt as a dog scents such things, and it will strengthen him. We must be equal to him, at the very least, in courage and determination.'

He smiled with sudden warmth. 'Aunt Mariah, you are the equal of anyone in determination, and I think in courage also.'

She blushed, something she had not done in years. Nothing on earth could stop her from living up to his estimation. She was too full of emotion even to thank him.

★ ★ ★

'Oh, no!' Rowena said, aghast, when they told her of their plan. 'I can't! I'd . . . ' Then she flushed pink.

They were in the sitting room beside the fire, fresh clothes and dry boots on, hot tea and shortbread on the table.

'Yes,' Mariah agreed. 'If you can't endure a little embarrassment in order to clear Cullen's name, and of course your own in the minds of those who imagine it was you who killed him

— and bring justice and some sense of resolution to the families that lost their daughters — not to mention preventing Durward from going on to do it again, and again — '

'He wouldn't!' Rowena said fiercely, and as soon as the words were out of her mouth the certainty vanished from her face, and a terrible fear took its place. 'Would he?' she whispered.

Mariah understood her fear in a more immediate and personal way.

'Men with appetites like that do not give them up, or perhaps I should say, leave them unfed, because of danger.'

'How would you know, Mariah?' Rowena asked.

It was Peter who intervened. 'I think that is information you do not need, Grandmother, but few lives pass without pain. What Aunt Mariah says is true. The only issue here is, are you with us, or against us? Must we do this alone?'

She stared at him in amazement, and dawning realisation that he meant exactly what he had said. She started to deny, then accepted the futility of it.

'So you will help?' he said. 'Good. Now we must plan it carefully. The only possible time is the Christmas Eve party the village holds every year. I know already that they have made their arrangements. All I need to do is tell the vicar that we are having one or two extra guests. He will be delighted.'

'Extra guests?' She looked puzzled.

'Yes. People from Brocklehurst who know what happened there, and have now the courage to come forward and speak. We need to make sure the Abbotts are going to be there. They deserve to know the truth.'

'But after all these years — ' Rowena began.

'Have you forgotten Grandfather?' he asked, his eyebrows raised. 'Or ceased to be hurt that people who used to be your friends, twenty years ago, and all your life before that, still believe that you could have killed him?'

'Peter! How can you say that to me?' Rowena was shocked.

'Because it is true,' he replied. 'And we are going to fight against it, and do everything possible to put it right.'

Rowena looked at Mariah. 'It is easy for you,' she said with a touch of bitterness. 'No one is going to rip away your privacy and laugh at you! No one . . . '

Again it was Peter who stopped her. 'Grandmother, you are being completely unfair. You. have no idea what Aunt Mariah may have given in order to get this matter admitted to, and persuade people to come forward. And neither do you actually know what griefs she may have suffered in her own life, far too deep to have told you about. You are being little better than the village gossip you so despise, leaping to conclusions about other people.'

Rowena was not only startled, she was now angry, a flush colouring her face.

'Peter! How dare you speak to me like that?'

'Because you need Aunt Mariah's help, and I am astounded that instead of gratitude, you are showing her only anger.'

Mariah could hardly believe what she seemed to be hearing. She was half driven to interrupt, but the half that admired Peter was stronger. It was the only time she could remember being praised in such a way. Now, please heaven, she must earn it.

She turned to Rowena. 'We cannot manage without you. One of the people who is coming from Brocklehurst gave witness to his presence with her at the time of the murder there . . . '

'Then he cannot have been guilty!' Rowena said immediately.

'Of course he can!' Mariah's resolution to keep her temper had not lasted long. 'She lied! She too had been . . . unwise . . . in her response to him and he exaggerated it, and threatened to tell her husband and the rest of the village that it had been far more than that. She did it to protect herself, and because she had never really accepted that he was guilty. Only when I told her of Christina Abbott, did she tell the truth. But she has the courage to come forward now.' She took a breath. 'If she is the only one, it will be easier to refute her. But when you say Durward used you too, it is a pattern. I dare say there may be others, similarly used, who will then realise they are not alone, and find the courage to come forward.'

There was a dawning understanding in Rowena's face. 'We could hurt him?' she said softly, almost under her breath.

'We must. If we don't, he will go on and kill other girls,' Mariah agreed.

Rowena shook her head.

'Yes,' Peter said bluntly. Then he leaned forward and kissed her cheek. 'Thank you, Grandmother. Now we must make all the arrangements so the village Christmas party accomplishes more than it ever has in all its long and happy past.'

★   ★   ★

Christmas Eve dawned cold and bright. It was one of those motionless days in winter when everything looks as if it were painted on glass. The frost was glittering sharp on every leaf and twig, but Mariah was too nervous to do more than notice its beauty in the odd moments as she passed a window.

Peter walked into the village to check at the inn, and returned to say that Bessie Collins was there, with her husband, the current constable of Brocklehurst, and also her father, the constable at the time of the child abduction and murder, twenty-five years ago. It took him some time to locate Mrs Johnson because she had chosen to stay with a friend. He noticed that she had come without her husband.

'She looked very tense,' he added quietly over luncheon. Welsh rarebit was very tasty. There was always something extraordinarily comforting about melted cheese on toast.

'Can we rely on her?' Rowena asked. Today she looked strong, even though it might well have cost her a considerable effort. Her hair was beautifully dressed, coiled up on her head, but not pulled tight. She had allowed its natural beauty to dictate its shape, and Mariah could not help admiring it. She hesitated. In their youth she had envied it. It always looked effortless, as if nothing in Rowena that was lovely were due to artifice.

Peter appeared oblivious to such things.

'I hope so,' she said a trifle ruefully. 'Perhaps if you were to go and call on her, she might find reassurance in it?'

Mariah could quite clearly see the fear in Rowena's face and then the resolve. She held her own peace.

'That would be a very good idea,' Rowena said after a moment. 'It is always better to know that you are not alone in a battle.'

Mariah smiled at her. 'Indeed. And we must be prepared for Durward to fight. He has a great deal to lose.'

'Not as much as the Abbotts lost,' Peter said drily, helping himself to another hot slice of toast and rich cheese sauce. 'I can just remember Christina, although she was four years older than I was. I think she was the first girl in whom I could see something to admire. I wasn't fond of girls then.' He smiled ruefully at remembrance of his childhood self. 'They weren't interested in the things that mattered, like railway engines or cricket. Especially, they weren't interested in cricket!'

'I shall go into the village as soon as we have finished luncheon,' Rowena said. 'In the meantime, I must think what to say to Mrs Johnson.'

'You must do as you please.' Mariah had not been asked, but she spoke anyway. 'But she

135

knows what the purpose is of our being here, so to disguise it might seem disingenuous. Trust might be a better way.'

'Thank you.' Instead of taking offence, Rowena sounded as if she were grateful for the advice. 'I would ask you to accompany me, but I fear she might feel a little outnumbered. And confidences are more easily shared with two, rather than three.'

'Of course,' Mariah agreed with relief. She wished to spend the afternoon with Peter, conferring on exactly how they were going to introduce the dangerous and very emotionally dark and powerful subject that would provoke the accusations that were their whole purpose in attending.

★　★　★

For the village Christmas party Rowena dressed in her very best. She was still a beautiful woman, when she wished to be. Her warm colouring was thrown into relief by the dark violet satin of her gown and her bare throat was flattered by a high, collar-style necklace, which hid the slight signs of ageing in her neck.

If envy had not been such a crippling emotion, Mariah might have allowed herself to envy her. She certainly had in the past. Now was different. Mariah would protect Rowena, for Cullen's sake, for Peter's, and also for her own sake. Mariah had never been beautiful, that was not a choice. Courage was, and she had fought for that, and won.

This evening she wore a dress of deep burgundy, a colour so rich it lent her face a glow it did not usually possess. It had been a gift from her granddaughter, Emily, who herself always dressed superbly, and she knew what suited everyone, even an elderly woman of no great stature or deportment, and whose hair had faded to an undistinguished grey.

And there was little time to fiddle with it in the glass now and make adjustments. It was time for battle.

They travelled in Rowena's small gig, but there was a good roof on it and the cold air did not swirl in through the isinglass windows. They arrived to find the village hall already well attended. But they were not so early as made one seem overeager.

Peter alighted immediately and offered his hand to his grandmother, then to Mariah. He gave Rowena an encouraging smile. He gripped Mariah's arm a little more warmly, almost like a discreet salute as they turned and walked up to the entrance.

The vicar greeted them without apparently noticing anything different from every year before. He had an excellent memory, and spoke to Mariah by name without prompting. But it flickered through her mind that perhaps word had already reached him of her rather unorthodox behaviour. Still, she smiled back at him and made some meaningless pleasantry, as if all were as usual.

Inside the hall were tables decked with food. There were scarlet candles lit and burning, garlands of leaves and ribbons, small silver-coloured bells and brass trumpets. A nativity scene sat on a table, replete with angels and farm animals as well. Here in a small village, the animals were particularly loved. Some of them were losing their fur where they had been too much stroked by small hands, unlike the figures of Mary and the Christ Child, which were too precious even to touch; they were simply gazed at with wonder, and perhaps even awe.

Mariah looked around her, filled with memories of this same hall, twenty years ago, and of other village church bells in the long past of her own childhood. She saw Mr and Mrs Abbott. They looked far more than twenty years older, and somehow smaller than she had remembered them. Grief seemed to have eaten away too much inside them.

Then she saw Owen Durward, tall, dark haired, his face as powerful, and as arrogant as always. And as if by some kind of magnetism, he turned and looked directly at her. For a moment their eyes were locked and it was a declaration of war. Then he smiled and the darkness vanished. He was too far away to speak to her without drawing attention to himself, but he inclined his head a little in acknowledgment of her, and smiled — or was it a baring of his teeth?

She smiled back, but charmingly, as if he did not disconcert her in the least. She would act as if she had won, right from the beginning, from the first shot, as it were.

The evening seemed to drag. Mariah saw Bessie Collins, and Mrs Johnson. Both seemed to her to look nervous. They remained together every occasion she saw them. But then in the same circumstances, if she had a friend who knew and understood her so well, she too would have remained as close as was seemly.

Mariah pretended to eat and enjoy the very generous food, but she found it hard to swallow even roast goose, tender and full of flavour though it was. She made trivial conversation, enquired after people's health and their families, and barely heard their replies.

Finally, Peter stood up at the slightly raised dais and rang his spoon on the crystal of his glass to request attention. After two or three attempts, everyone fell silent and turned to face him.

'Ladies and gentlemen, friends,' he began. He stood under the light, with its warmth shining on his fair hair and his handsome face, suitably grave for the occasion. 'It is twenty years since my grandfather, Cullen Wesley, died. I think all of you here knew him. I would like to raise a glass of this excellent wine in remembrance of his life, his love of this village and its people, and the services he performed for many of you.'

He hesitated.

Mariah willed him not to lose his nerve. Would he even be aware of her, and her mind so focused on him?

'And also, in an even sadder remembrance,' Peter continued, holding his glass so the light caught in it facets and made it sparkle. 'I would ask you to think of Christina Abbott. She was one of us. We lost her to an atrocity that has never been resolved.'

139

He smiled with intense sorrow. 'I was only ten when that happened. You may think it was of little meaning to me. You would be wrong. At ten I didn't have much time for girls. They didn't play cricket. They weren't interested in guns or swords, or making model ships. They didn't play at fighting. In fact, to me they weren't much use for anything, except teasing, if you dared to.'

There was a murmur of understanding, a little nervous laughter.

'But Christina could tie the rigging on a model ship better than any boy,' he went on, his voice thick with emotions he did not attempt to hide. 'And she could play the piano and made real music on it, not just scales up and down. She loved it, and you could tell that just by listening. You didn't even have to see the smile on her face.'

Mrs Abbott was staring at him with tears on her cheeks.

Mariah could see the grief in other people too, women unashamed to show it, men trying to pretend they were stronger, when clearly it touched them just as much.

Peter went on quickly, 'And she was pretty good at getting Cook to give her jam tarts, enough of them to share with hungry boys. I know, because I was one of those boys. And she was good at sums, better than I was. She was the first girl who spoke to me sensibly and made me realise that it was quite possible that one day I would actually like girls.'

Mariah looked across the room at Durward.

140

He appeared uncomfortable. Or did she just imagine that?

'Actually, I already liked Christina,' Peter went on, now also struggling to keep his composure. 'I wasn't going to cry when they told me she was dead. Somebody had actually hurt her badly, and then killed her, so she wouldn't tell on them. At least I wasn't going to cry where anyone could see me. But my grandfather knew, and he said it was all right to be more upset than you could hide when something really bad happened. It was bad then, it's still bad.' He looked around the crowd as if seeking someone in particular. 'And I didn't know until this Christmas that something almost exactly the same happened five years before that in Brocklehurst, only forty miles away. Another girl was taken, raped and murdered . . . '

There was a ripple of anger and dismay around the room. A man called out somewhere in protest.

'Of course you are angry!' Peter agreed. 'No, it isn't a nice subject to raise at Christmas. It isn't nice to raise it at all. But that crime was never solved either. Are we going to choose Christmas to tell her parents not to spoil our enjoyment by saying they still hurt? And it still matters!'

The vicar pulled at Peter's sleeve and Peter ignored him.

'Constable Harris!' Peter went on, staring at the retired constable from Brocklehurst. 'You thought, twenty-five years ago, that Owen Durward was guilty. But Mrs Johnson told you that he could not be, because she could swear to

141

his whereabouts at the time.'

Constable Harris nodded.

Everyone turned to stare at him.

He moved forward, pushing people aside to stand next to Peter.

'That's right,' he agreed, facing the crowd. 'She believed he was innocent, and she was prepared to lie to save him. And she's told me since then that she was foolish enough to flirt with him. He threatened to tell not only her husband, but the whole village, that it had been far more than a mere flirtation. He was the town doctor. He would have been believed. He would tell things about her that only a lover, or a doctor, would know.'

Now there were calls of outrage from a few people, but they were immediately silenced by others. Many turned to look at Mrs Johnson, and she stood, scarlet faced, tears in her eyes, but she did not deny it.

Rowena pushed her way through the crowd until she stood on the other side of Peter.

'I know how she feels,' she said, her voice wobbling but heard quite clearly, at least by those closest to her. 'Because I made the same mistake. I let Dr Durward do the same thing to me, and I behaved foolishly. I was not intimate with him ... ' She clearly found the words difficult to say, and her face was burning with colour. 'He rebuffed what he thought was an advance. It wasn't! But I found him dangerous, and so also attractive. And I was ashamed of that. He played on my embarrassment, and told my husband. Or at least that is what he said to me. He even said that that was the reason Cullen had declined to act as his lawyer when he was charged with having abducted — ' she swallowed and almost choked — 'and raped Christina; that my husband would not defend him because I had so clearly found him compellingly attractive.'

There was now a considerable noise in the gathered throng.

Surprisingly, for a woman so obviously humiliated, Rowena raised her voice above them.

'That was not the reason! My grandson, Peter, discovered that my husband went to Brocklehurst the day before he resigned from the case. He learned about the other murder, of Mary Catherwood, which in every particular was the same as Christina's. She too was taken, violated, and then killed. Owen Durward was suspected, but a married woman, whom he had said was attracted to him, foolishly, embarrassingly so, prevented his being charged. Just as it looked as if my action had prevented my husband from defending him. The following day, Cullen was murdered and the question was raised that it was I who had killed him, because of my . . . my ill-judged behaviour with Durward.'

Peter put his arm around Rowena and hugged her quickly, then let her go. 'We could not stop it before,' he said loudly, looking directly at Owen Durward. 'But if it happens again, and it will, then we will be to blame, because we did not stop it now. Durward has been tried and found not guilty of killing Christina Abbott so he cannot be tried again, whatever proof we find. But he was never charged with killing Mary

Catherwood. The law will forget some crimes, after long enough time has passed, but never the rape and murder of a child! Neither will we forget!'

One by one the people's hands were raised in agreement, almost all men, except one or two slender arms wrapped in velvet and silk. Mariah sensed the mood shift quickly and dangerously from interest to anger, and possibly violence.

Several men looked towards Durward, and it was perfectly clear that they believed both Mrs Johnson and Rowena. Two or three of them closed in on Durward, who took a few steps closer to the door, his face distorted with rage. He snatched a wine glass and broke the end of it against a table.

One of the men stopped, holding back the others.

Mariah held her breath.

There was a sudden scuffle. Durward lunged sideways with the broken glass in his hand. There was a shriek, sharp with pain and outrage, then a man toppled, blood on his white shirt front. He fell, taking two more people down with him as they lost their balance.

A woman screamed.

Durward started to run.

Mariah was about the same distance from the door as he was, but her way was clear. She picked up her skirts and bent forward, moving rapidly. She reached the door ahead of him and picked up a dish of blancmange from one of the side tables, intending to strike him with it, if it proved necessary to stop his escape. She swung around to face him, but Durward charged towards her, knocking a woman aside. She realised that she was not strong enough to stop him, so she flung it on to the floor. The white jellylike pudding hurtled off and landed in front of him. His feet hit it and flew out from under him. He landed hard on his back, knocking the wind out of his body. Mariah heard his head strike the boards. He lay still.

A moment later, Peter stood there. He looked at Durward lying motionless. Then he saw the blancmange on the floor, and the skid marks, and Mariah still holding the bowl.

'I knew he wouldn't escape you, Aunt Mariah!' he said jubilantly. 'You don't give up, not ever.' He stepped forward and put his arms around her, holding her tightly.

Constable Harris walked up to them and stood over Durward. He prodded him with his foot. Durward groaned.

Peter walked across, took one of the curtain cords and handed it to the constable, who then jerked Durward's hands behind his back and tied them tight and hard.

'Owen Durward, I am arresting you for the rape and murder of Mary Catherwood. Now come quietly, don't spoil everyone's Christmas party. They've a right to celebrate, to remember birth and death, people they've loved and lost, and that because of Christmas, love never dies.' He looked at Mariah, and the mess on the floor. 'Thank you, Mrs Ellison. Quick thinking.'

'Oh, she did much more than that,' Peter said firmly. 'Durward never had a chance. Aunt

145

Mariah never gives up. Not ever. As you said, love never dies. Neither does courage, nor hope. Happy Christmas, Constable.'

'Happy Christmas, Mr Wesley, Aunt Mariah. Sorry . . . Mrs Ellison.'

'Aunt Mariah is fine,' she replied. 'And happy Christmas to you.'

SHOULDER THE SKY
ANGELS IN THE GLOOM
AT SOME DISPUTED BARRICADE
WE SHALL NOT SLEEP